Obsession

Jayne Osborne

Barbara Shaw

Published by FeedARead.com

A CIP catalogue record for this title is available from the British Library.

Dedicated to my husband

Chapter One

Francesca Hallett stared around the empty room, remembering how it had been furnished, and wondering whether she would ever see her home again. She had been bought up here, and after her mother had passed away, she had never envisaged leaving it, but older and wiser heads had prevailed, and she was having to go. Now she drew in a deep breath, and went around the house again, making sure that everything had been taken, and nothing had been left. The only thing left now, was the case, containing the last of her possessions, packed and waiting in the hallway. Tears filled her eyes as she stared around her, but she wiped them away with her hand, and shut the door of the sitting room. The new owners would be moving in very soon, and she didn't want to be around when they came. Her sister and brother had dealt with everything to do with the house move, and not wanting to see the people who had wanted to see round it, she had always left the viewings in the hands of the estate agent. Although she now had enough money to buy a flat of her own, she had not decided where she wanted to live, so not wanting to have to leave the house in a rush, two months before, she had moved into the nurses home, only going back to the house occasionally, to collect any post, and to make sure that everything was in order, before the house sale was completed. There was a ring at the door bell, and she knew it was the taxi she had ordered, so went to the front door, picking up the case as she went, and the driver took it from her and put it in the back of the car. She like her sister, who had inherited her fathers' good looks, his blonde hair and his height, and nobody believed that they were sisters, when they first met, and her brother was equally as tall, and slim, and was thought by her friends, to be quite handsome. She sighed again, and with a glance at her watch, went down to supper.

The dining room was crowded and she stood, her tray in her hands, as she looked around for somewhere to sit. She caught sight of her sister, who was sitting with some friends, and was waved across to join her. Francesca sat down at the table, and started to eat, exchanging greetings with her sister's friends as she did so, but they got up and left before Francesca had finished eating. "Did everything go okay?" Samantha asked her, when they were alone, and she nodded. "The furniture van came early this morning, and took everything that was left, away. It was odd, seeing the house without anything in it" she replied. "I made sure that everything had gone, left notes about where the electricity meter and the gas taps were, indicated where the stop tap for the water supply was, then the taxi came, and I locked up, put the keys through the letter box, then came back here."
"You were good to do that" her sister told her. "I couldn't get any time off, and goodness knows what Andy was doing. I saw him in the corridor for a minute, this morning, but he didn't stop, just waved and was gone. You know what he's like at the moment."
"Yes, he'll have a new consultant to deal with soon

as well, and it must be stressful for him. I wonder how he's going to react to being a father?" she smiled as she thought of her brother's face when he had told them that his wife was pregnant. She didn't get on with her sister-in-law very well. Theresa was ambitious for Andrew, pushing him to better himself all the time, and not the kind of person she had ever envisaged Andy ending up with. Still, she thought, Andy was happy with Theresa, and she had no doubt that the other woman would be quite a good mother. She had been one of the people who had really wanted the house to be sold, knowing that her husband would benefit from quite a nice sum of money, as his share of the property. She obviously hadn't cared that selling the house would leave Francesca without anywhere to call home, and had pushed Andy into persuading Samantha that they ought to sell it. She pushed her plate away, and sat back in the chair. Sam glanced at her watch and stood up. "I'm due back on duty" she said now, "I'll be off tomorrow evening. Do you want to come and have a meal?"

"Can't" said Francesca, "I'm doing a split duty, so my off duty will be in the middle of the day. Sister said they don't have enough staff, and I'm not doing anything, so I agreed to change." She grinned at her sister, "I'll give you a ring sometime." she said, and waved farewell as the other girl hurried away back to the ward, where she was a senior staff nurse on a medical unit. Francesca gathered together her sister's dirty crockery, piled it on the tray, and placed it on the rack, before she walked slowly back to her room.

She was sitting at the desk in her room, writing up some notes, when there was a knock at the door, and when it opened, she found Ally, her best friend on the threshold. "I thought you might be back" Ally said now, "How's things? Was it odd, handing over the keys?"

"Didn't see anybody." she said now, ushering Ally in, and shutting the door behind her. Ally sat on the bed, and Francesca closed her notebook and placed it back on the desk. She had lifted the kettle, filled it with water, and was making a cup of tea for them both, as she spoke. "Just made sure that the house was clear and nothing had been left behind, wrote notes telling the new owner where the meters were, and where to turn off things like water and gas, and then locked up and put the keys through the door. I don't think I could have coped with meeting the new owners. It was bad enough knowing that it had been sold." She smiled sadly at her friend, and changed the subject "What about you? Did Sister say anything about Mr. Baldwin's dressing?"

Ally shook her head. "Not one word. She must have known that Celia had said she could do it, and then didn't, so I had to do it instead of her, but she didn't say a thing. At report this morning she just said that dressings were to be allocated by Staff Davies, but nothing else. Honestly Fran, I can't stand Celia. She gets told to do things, but always manages to duck out of doing them by saying she doesn't know how to do them, and is never around when somebody else does it, so she can be shown how to do something. I know I've shown her how to do Mr.

Baldwin's dressing twice at least." Francesca nodded. "I thought you had." she agreed. "I've shown her twice as well." Ally nodded. "We weren't like that when we were in our first year, were we? If we didn't know how to do something, we said so, and we got taught that way. Celia doesn't, she just accepts everything she's told to do, then doesn't do it, and we have to rush round after her, doing her job as well as own. Goodness knows what she's going to be like if she's on the ward and there's an emergency. But Sister doesn't say a word. We won't get asked for our opinion, when Sister has to write the report, but you can bet your bottom dollar, that she'll talk to Staff Davies about her, and I really hope that Staff tells her what a useless person Celia is. The girl should never have been allowed to start her training." she grinned at her friend, "Did you know that she fainted the first time she was asked to assist with a colostomy bag change?"
"No" said Francesca, her eyes alight with laughter. "What happened, and when was that?"
"Her first ward" Ally replied, "apparently the nurse doing the dressing had to yell for help, to get her off the floor, because she couldn't see to her and to the patient as well." She grinned, "I only heard that today. One of the nurses in the canteen told me. Everybody at our table was laughing about it, when she'd finished telling the story."
"I wonder what Miss Lines will do, if she gets another bad report?" Francesca asked, and Ally shook her head. "Well, if she gets three bad reports from three different wards, then they'll probably ask her to leave." she said, and the girls were silent. The

girl in question was petite, very pretty, with curly blonde hair and blue eyes, which she used to good effect on the junior medical staff, but Ally was right, the girl should never have been allowed to start her training in the first place. Francesca sighed. "Have you written up your last lot of lecture notes yet?" she asked, and Ally shook her head. "I was going to do them tomorrow." she admitted, "Have you?"

"I was just doing them now. Go and get yours, and we can do them together. Honestly, I don't know why we have to do them, especially as we're waiting for our results." Ally sighed and nodded. "I quite agree." she said now, "Finish making the tea, and I'll get my notebooks." She went out of the room, to return soon with her notebooks, and very soon, the two girls were engrossed in their work. They had finished them, and drunk the teapot dry, when Ally suddenly sat up. "Did you hear?" she said, "They've finally appointed somebody to take Mr. Barker's place. Apparently, he was appointed a couple of weeks ago, and he'll be starting in about five weeks' time. Just when we get our results, so we don't know if we'll be working with him or not. Dave Brewster told me that he's going to be looking around the hospital for a while, before he gets down to work. Wonder what he's going to be like?"

"I have no idea" Francesca said. "I'm just hoping he's going to be nice to student nurses" she laughed. "I know we should be qualified soon, but we're still going to be students for the next few weeks, we'll continue to be students if we fail our exams, and if he decides he doesn't like student nurses, it could be rather tricky working on the

ward."
"He might be very nice" Ally said, but Francesca shook her head. "I thought you were settled quite happily with Simon?" she queried, and Ally grinned at her friend. "I am," she replied, "but there's no harm in looking, even if I don't touch" Francesca laughed at her friends' comments then yawned. "I'm going to chuck you out and go to bed" she said, "It's been a long day for me, up early, making sure that the house was cleared, and I'm on another split tomorrow because some of us have got a day off." and she looked meaningfully at her friend, because Ally was going to be on a day off. "Another one?" Ally said "You're doing too many split duties. Why do you always have to do them?"
"Because Sister knew that Aileen wouldn't be back on duty until Friday, and she's going to be short of staff. I'm going to be on with Mary and Justine. My only problem is that Celia is on tomorrow evening as well. I'm probably going to have to do her work, as well as mine."
"Good luck" her friend replied, as she gathered together her notebooks and mug. "I'll see you sometime tomorrow," and left the room. Francesca nodded, and started to prepare for her bed. As she had told Ally, she was tired, and knew she had a long day on the following day, so she was soon tucked up in her bed, the light was out, and as she settled into sleep, her last thought was to hope that the new man would be kind.

The following day started well – when she went off duty, for a few hours after the morning shift, she

understand you're waiting for your final results. No wonder you were left in charge last night. Sister must rate you highly, to give you that amount of responsibility."
"I'm doing well, thank you." she said, "and I was only in charge last night, because one of the staff nurses was off sick, and Sister couldn't rearrange the off duty to have one of the others on duty, so I did a split duty. And then the girl who was going to be in charge was taken away by one of the other wards who didn't have any staff at all."
"Complicated" he said with a smile. "So where are you off to now?"
"I'm going back to the ward" she replied. "I had to go and see the nursing officer about something that happened last night- she needed to know the full details, and while I was there, she told me that if I pass my exams, then I've got the job I wanted."
"Congratulations" he said "where do you want to work?"
"Theatres" she answered him with a smile. "I really loved my time there when I did my placement, and the Sister told me I'd be most welcome if I wanted to go back. Don't get me wrong, I like being able to talk to my patients when they're awake, but I like the idea of working in theatres."
"Well, good for you" he said. "I hope you'll be very happy."
"Thank you" she said, and then "I'd better go. I might see you on the ward, but in the meantime, please give your father my best wishes."
"I will do" he nodded, and she went on her way. He appeared to be very friendly, and she felt at ease

ward."
"He might be very nice" Ally said, but Francesca shook her head. "I thought you were settled quite happily with Simon?" she queried, and Ally grinned at her friend. "I am," she replied, "but there's no harm in looking, even if I don't touch" Francesca laughed at her friends' comments then yawned. "I'm going to chuck you out and go to bed" she said, "It's been a long day for me, up early, making sure that the house was cleared, and I'm on another split tomorrow because some of us have got a day off." and she looked meaningfully at her friend, because Ally was going to be on a day off. "Another one?" Ally said "You're doing too many split duties. Why do you always have to do them?"
"Because Sister knew that Aileen wouldn't be back on duty until Friday, and she's going to be short of staff. I'm going to be on with Mary and Justine. My only problem is that Celia is on tomorrow evening as well. I'm probably going to have to do her work, as well as mine."
"Good luck" her friend replied, as she gathered together her notebooks and mug. "I'll see you sometime tomorrow," and left the room. Francesca nodded, and started to prepare for her bed. As she had told Ally, she was tired, and knew she had a long day on the following day, so she was soon tucked up in her bed, the light was out, and as she settled into sleep, her last thought was to hope that the new man would be kind.

The following day started well – when she went off duty, for a few hours after the morning shift, she

was able to have a meal and relax before she went back on duty. She had changed out of her uniform and run to the local shops, to purchase a few necessities for herself, and was on her way back, when she ran around the corner, and collided with a very large man walking towards her. He was tall, dark haired, broadly built and beside him she felt very small. "Watch it" he said, and he put out his arms to stop her, as she came to a halt in front of him. "Sorry" she apologised. "I was in a bit of a hurry. I hope I didn't hurt you."
"No," he said, "there's not enough of you to hurt me. Are you okay?"
"Yes, I'm fine thanks." She stepped aside, "Will you excuse me please?" and without waiting for an answer, she ran across the forecourt of the hospital, and around the corner of the building towards the nurses home. She was watched by the man she had collided with, who was smiling as he watched her go.

Two hours later, very neat in her uniform, she made her way back to the ward she was working on, wondering what the evening held. She was on duty with Celia, a part time staff nurse - Mary Delaney, and an auxiliary nurse, Justine, both very experienced and as such liable to be borrowed by another ward, if they were short of staff. She entered the office and took the report from Sister, wondering where Mary Delaney was, because she couldn't see her, but at the finish, Sister didn't move. "I don't like leaving you on your own with Celia" she said. "I know there's a problem, but I don't have the staff to be able to put more people on duty, and I'm really sorry,

but Mary Delaney, has been reallocated to work elsewhere this evening. Apparently one of the other wards, is even shorter of staff, than we are, so Miss Lines told me, when she phoned. So, I'm afraid, you're going to be in charge. Do you reckon you'll be able to cope, or would you like me to tell Miss Lines, that I need Mary to stay with you?"
"I'll be okay Sister. Justine's here isn't she, and she's as good as another nurse. If I'm in dire straits, I'll phone the Office and ask for assistance, but I'm sure I'll be okay."
"It's up to you Francesca" Sister said as she rolled down her sleeves. "Thank you for splitting your duty. I do appreciate it, you know that. I meant to ask before, when do you get your exam results? And where have you applied to work?"
"We get our results in five weeks' time, and I've applied for theatre or surgical work. I really liked theatres when I worked there, so if there are any vacancies, I'm hoping they might accept me."
"Oh, they would definitely accept you" Sister said, with a smile. "They're always desperate for staff, or so I've been told. But I meant to tell you, Mr. Barker's replacement has been appointed, but I haven't been told what his name is yet. He's meant to be coming to do a tour of the hospital, before he starts work, so you'll probably meet him when he comes in. I do hope you have a quiet evening, Francesca. I'll see you tomorrow."
"Thanks Sister. See you then." She watched as the other woman left the office, and went to assist Celia and Justine with the evening chores. Between them, they gave out meals, assisted a couple of the

patients to eat them, made sure that everything was done properly, and got the ward ready for evening visitors. There weren't many of them waiting to be admitted, and when she opened the ward doors to show they were ready for visitors, there wasn't the rush that normally happened. Presumably, there had been a lot of visitors in the afternoon, she thought, as she sent Justine to take a well-earned coffee break. She was walking down the ward, after talking to a relative, when she saw Celia, shaking one of the patients. "Fran" she called. "There's something wrong with Mr. Daniels" and Francesca swiftly walked over to the old man. "What happened?" she asked, as she tried to find the old man's pulse, but Celia couldn't answer her properly. "He isn't talking to me" she said softly, and Fran registered that the old man wasn't breathing properly and didn't have a recognisable pulse, so hurriedly pulled the curtains around him. "Go and ring for the crash team" she instructed Celia, but the girl just stood there. "For goodness sake Celia, go and ring for help" she snapped, as she pulled the pillows out from under the old man's head, and started artificial resuscitation. The younger girl just stood where she was, staring at her, and Fran, knowing she was on her own, pulled the emergency cord, and hoped that Justine would hear it. She did, and appeared swiftly. She looked in, realised what was happening, and left the cubicle, reappearing a couple of seconds later with the crash trolley, and pushed Celia away. "Go away" she said, and shut the curtains fully, so that the visitors couldn't see what was happening. Fran was applying resuscitation, and it seemed an age,

before the crash team arrived to take over from her. Justine had left the cubicle, but Fran stayed where she was. It seemed a long time, before the anaesthetist on the team pronounced that the old man seemed to be getting better. “I think we'll take him to ITU” he said, and Fran went to make the arrangements for his transfer. Celia was nowhere to be seen, but Justine was keeping an eye on the ward, and smiled at her, as she went back behind the curtains. “The porters are coming” she told the anaesthetist, and he nodded. “Are you short of staff tonight, Fran?” he asked, and she nodded. “I'll say,” she replied. “Barmouth Ward pinched Mary Daniels, because they've got no staff, I'm doing a split today anyway, and I'm on with Justine, who's as good as a trained nurse anyway, and Celia, who is a first year, and doesn't seem to have a clue as to what to do. I think I'm going to have to have a word with Sister tomorrow about her,” The anaesthetist smiled at her, “well, you did okay. I think he owes his life to you. What about his family?”
“I've got his details in the office, if anybody could be spared to talk to them, before he goes to ITU. I think it would come better from a trained person, rather than me.” The doctor who was monitoring the old man's pulse rate nodded. “I’ll get somebody to phone them from ITU” he said. “Are they local, do we know?” Francesca nodded. “I think so, I'll go and get his notes ready to take to ITU with him, and we can check,” and she left the cubicle again. She was collecting the notes together, when the man she had bumped into that afternoon reached the office doorway. “Hello” she smiled at him, “Can I help

you?" she enquired and he smiled in return. "Yes, I've come to visit Mr. Daniels, but I can see his curtains have been pulled round him. Is there a problem?"
"I'm afraid so. May I ask who you are?"
"Certainly, I'm his son, Dominic." Francesca smiled at him. "Would you mind waiting for a minute, and I'll get somebody to come and talk to you." He nodded and she went past him, and into the cubicle again. "That's good timing" she said, "his son is here to see him, so if somebody would like to talk to him now, they could go up to ITU together." The anaesthetist nodded. "I'll go" he announced. "Where is he?"
"By the office door" she replied, and continued her work, gathering together Mr. Daniel's belongings so they could be taken to ITU with him. The anaesthetist arrived back, together with the porters, and smiled at her. "He's going to go and wait outside ITU, until we're ready to let him see him. If everything is ready, I'll take him up." Francesca smiled at him. He was a very nice man, happily married, but always considerate to the nurses, and they all got on well with him. Once the patient had been transferred to the Intensive Therapy Unit, she pulled the curtains back, and looked around the ward. Justine had rung the bell to signify the end of visiting hours, and the ward was quiet once more, but there was no sign of Celia. "Where is she?" Francesca asked Justine, and the other woman nodded towards the sluice. "She's probably crying her eyes out in there" she said. "She went to pieces when I rushed past her, when you rang the panic

bell, and I haven't really seen her since." She looked at Francesca, "Shall I go and find her and tell her to get on with making the bed up?"
"If you wouldn't mind" Francesca said, and went back to the ward to make sure that the rest of the patients were okay. There was nothing needed from her, and she looked up as Justine came towards her.
"I can't find her" she said. "Her cloaks gone from the cupboard. It looks like she ran away, and took everything with her."
"You're joking!" Francesca was very angry with the younger girl. "I'll have to talk to Sister tomorrow, and something will have to be done about her. She can't just pack up and go home, when something has upset her." she smiled at the other woman. "The night staff will be here soon, so shall we get that bed made up before they come, and then if you wouldn't mind keeping an eye on the ward while I give the report, we can both get off duty. Thanks." she said as she went to get some linen to remake the bed that was empty, and came back to find Justine wiping the cover of the mattress. They swiftly finished the chore, as the night nurses came on duty, and she went into the office to give the handover report. It was longer than normal, because she had to give details of Mr. Daniels collapse and transfer to the other unit, and by the time she had come to the end and said her farewells, she was looking forward to nothing more than a cup of tea and her bed. She and Justine walked along the corridor together, until they came to the intersection of the corridors, where Justine would go one way, and she would take the other, to go towards the nurses home, and they

stopped. “Thanks Justine” Francesca said, “I couldn't have managed this evening without you” but the other woman shook her head. “You'd have coped” she said. “I'll see you tomorrow” and she walked away. Francesca had just taken a few steps along the corridor, when a voice behind her made her turn around. “I understand I have to thank you for my father's life” and there standing in front of her, was the man who had come to the office that evening. “No” she said, “I assisted, but the hard work was done by the team who looked after him. How is he now?”

“He's doing fine thanks. They'll be keeping him in the unit for a day or so, but Dr. Bryant told me that you'd already got his heart going again, by the time they got to the ward.” She looked down at her feet. “Well, yes,” she admitted, “but they did all the hard work.”

“So you said.” he remarked. “But I wanted to say thanks to you and your staff for being so quick witted.”

“Thanks” she said, then as the silence continued, “would you excuse me please, I'm just going off duty now.”

“I will. I just wondered what your name was?”

“I'm Nurse Hallett” she replied, and wasn't really surprised when he asked for her first name. “It's Francesca” she admitted. “Well, thank you again Francesca” he said. “I'm Dominic Cavanagh. Goodnight”.

“Goodnight” she said, and turned to walk away. She became aware that he hadn't moved. “I'm sure we'll see each other again.” he said, then finally, he turned

and walked away.
Francesca walked slowly back to the nurses home, and alone at last in her room, pulled off her cape, cap and took off her shoes, before putting the kettle on to boil.

She was sitting drinking a cup of tea, and eating a biscuit, when the door opened, and Ally entered. "How was it?" she asked. "Did she play you up?"
Francesca nodded and told her friend about that evening's events. "I'll have to talk to Sister about it." she said finally, "she can't do that again, just grabbing her cloak and going without a word to anybody. I'll bet she tries to make it out that it was my fault, as well."
"Don't fret" Ally reassured her friend. "I think that Sister knows what she's like, and she really wouldn't have been keen on leaving you on duty with her, especially when Mary Delaney was taken away. But Fran, what I wanted to tell you, was the news I got given at supper time. Mr. Barker's replacement has been seen, and apparently, he's got everybody who's met him, in a bit of a spin. He's tall, dark and handsome, and unmarried to boot."
"How on earth did anybody find that out?" Francesca asked "What he looks like doesn't have any bearing on how good he is at his job, does it?"
Ally nodded. "No, but it does help, doesn't it? We'll probably meet him if he comes to do a round. He's going to spend the next few weeks just catching up with everything that Mr. Barker was doing, before he left. The girls in theatre were saying they've met him already and he was very pleasant to them.

Apparently, Sister Lewis was all over him, all the theatre girls were really surprised at the way she acted, because she's never shown any interest in any of the other men, but as somebody said, him being good looking, well that made it even better."

"Ally, give over do." Francesca begged her friend. "As you say, we'll meet him when he comes to the ward, but we won't have anything to do with him will we? Sister will be looking after him, and we'll be banished to do dressings or something so we won't be in the ward. But I meant to tell you, Sister asked me where I'd applied to work, and when I told her I'd asked for theatres, she said they'd welcome me with open arms. I'm hoping she's right."

"You always did like theatres" Ally said, then saw her friends face. "Okay, I'm going, so you can get to bed. I'm on a late tomorrow, so I'll see you at lunchtime. Have a good sleep won't you"

"Thanks Ally. Did you have a good day?" Ally nodded, but didn't give her any details, and she smiled, for she had probably spent the day with her fiancée, Simon. "See you tomorrow" she said, and Francesca watched as her friend left the room. She prepared for bed, after having a swift bath, and as she lay back against the pillows, she remembered the man who had thanked her for saving his father's life. What had he said his name was? She remembered then, Dominic - that was quite a nice name. He had been quite nice too, she thought to herself, and had said he was sure they would meet again. She smiled to herself, closed her eyes, and was soon asleep.

Chapter Two

The following morning, the ward was hectic and Francesca was kept busy. She had been able to have coffee on the ward, and she was returning from her break, when Sister called her into the office. "So, what happened last night Fran?" she asked. "I hear from Justine that Celia lost her head, but I need to know exactly."

Francesca sighed as she told Sister Ellis precisely what she had said and done. "I asked her to go and get the crash team, and she didn't move, so I told her again to go and get help. She didn't move, so I pressed the panic bell, Justine came running, and she told Celia to go away, and I stayed with the team. It was only when we were going to get the bed ready, after Mr. Daniels had been taken to ITU, that we tried to find her, and she wasn't to be seen. Justine said that her cloak had gone as well, so we assumed she went when we were trying to resuscitate Mr. Daniels. She'd been fine during the evening – okay she's a bit slow, but I didn't have any problem with her."

Sister Ellis nodded. "Don't worry Fran, you did everything right. The crash team said that you were very calm throughout the entire procedure. Was that your first arrest?"

"No, I've seen a couple now" she answered, "but they never get any easier, do they?" The older woman smiled at her. "No, they don't" she smiled, "but after the first one, you just snap into action and go into automatic mode." She nodded to herself. "Don't worry about things Fran. I'm going to have a talk with Miss Lines, and I think that Celia will be

much happier when she's not nursing anymore." she sighed. "Off you go and get on with the dressings if you wouldn't mind. I believe the new surgeon might be coming to visit the ward soon. I'll have to introduce you."
"Thanks Sister, but it's not necessary. I'll meet him sooner or later."
"Off you go then Fran. And thanks for doing the split yesterday. I did appreciate it, but I'm going to make certain that I don't have to ask you to do any more."
Francesca went back to her work, doing the dressings on the patients on the ward. She had been told that Mr. Daniels was doing well, and was glad, for she liked the old man. He was always cheerful, even after his surgery for a fractured hip, and she had never seen him downhearted. She was laying up a trolley in the dressing room, prior to going to see to one of the patients, when she heard a commotion, and seeing the nursing officer approaching, realised that Miss Lines was accompanying a tall man, who was bending to listen to what she said. Francesca looked through the glass of the door and knew she would be able to stay in the dressing room until Miss Lines left. She got on well with the nursing officer, but if she was taking the new surgeon on a tour of the hospital, she didn't want to get in her way. She saw the two Staff nurses enter the office and pull the door closed behind them, and knew she would go and dress Mr. Evans wound instead, so without looking at the group of people in the office, she pushed the trolley into the ward, and into Mr. Evans cubicle, pulling the curtains behind her. She could hear talking, as Sister took the group round the

ward, but because she was behind curtains, she was not interrupted, and she could clearly hear Sister Ellis saying goodbye to her visitors. When she had finished the dressing, she cleared the trolley and went back to the dressing room, to get ready for the next patient, and was waylaid by Sister. "Oh Fran" she said, her eyes sparkling, "what a fascinating man. I'm sorry I wasn't able to introduce you, but you were behind curtains, but I'm sure you'll meet him sooner or later. He's our new consultant. His speciality is Orthopaedics, obviously, but he's got a few good ideas, about what he'd like to do, and get on with, but he wanted to meet the ward staff, because he'll be working with us, so he wants to be able to put faces to names. He's not starting to operate for a while, but I'm sure you will meet him later when it's convenient."
Francesca nodded. "I'll go and finish off if that's okay Sister?" she said, and the other woman smiled at her. "Okay Fran. Dinners will be up in a while, so make sure you've finished before they come up won't you. When the late staff come on duty, make sure you have a break, because I was told that you didn't even manage to get a cup of tea yesterday, so you're owed time for your supper break as well." She smiled at the other girl. "ITU phoned and said they're going to send Mr. Daniels back tomorrow, if he's still making good progress."
"I'm glad," said Francesca. "He's such a nice man, and I really hope he'll be able to get well and go home soon."
"Off you go then" said Sister, and Francesca went to finish the dressings. As the senior student nurse, she

did a lot of the patient's dressings, for Sister realised she knew what she was about, and had no compunction in using her skills.

That afternoon, during visiting time, she was able to have a leisurely cup of tea, knowing that one of the Staff Nurses was in the ward, along with Ally, and a couple of other staff. There had been no sign of Celia all day, and as far as she knew, there had been no message from her, and she wondered what Miss Lines had said when Sister told her about the events of the previous evening. She looked up as one of the auxiliaries came into the kitchen, and told her that she was to go and see the Nursing Officer, and knew it was going to be about the previous evening. Sister Ellis looked up from her paperwork, as she went to tell her that she was going, and smiled at her. "Don't worry Fran" she said, "she just wants your account of what happened. Celia won't be coming back, but she needs to know exactly what happened. Justine has already been to see her, and now she wants your side of the story." Francesca walked swiftly to the Nursing Officers Office, and knocked on the door. When she was admitted, it was as Sister had told her, all Miss Lines wanted to know was what had happened. "Thank you, Francesca," she said eventually "That will be all. Oh, before you go, I just wanted to let you know that if you do pass your exams, then Theatres will be glad to have you on their staff. I will be speaking to all the girls who took their exams, and are now awaiting results, but as you are here, I thought I'd let you know now."

"Thanks Miss Lines." Francesca smiled at the other woman. "I just hope I pass the exams now. The waiting for the results is a worrying time, as I'm sure you realise" The nursing officer nodded. "I can well remember having to wait for my results" she said, "I don't think I was very good company during the eight weeks it took for the results to come through. But don't worry my dear, I'm sure you've done well. Your previous exam results were very encouraging, so I don't think there is much to worry about. You'd better go back to your ward now Fran."
Francesca nodded, and turned to go out of the door, when the woman spoke again. "Are you settling in well into the nurses home?" she asked softly, "I know what an upheaval it is, when you sell a house."
"Thank you yes" said Francesca, but the other woman said nothing else, and she walked back along the corridors that would lead to the wards. She was passing the doorway of the Intensive Care Unit, when a man exited, and she had to move out of his way, before they collided. "Sorry" she gasped, then smiled as she recognised Mr. Daniels son. "Oh hello" he said, smiling back at her. "Sorry, I wasn't looking where I was going."
"How's your father?" she asked "We were told he might be coming back to us soon, if he continues to improve."
"That's right" the man said. "He's doing very well, getting stronger by the minute, and complaining that the nurses on the Unit aren't as pretty as the ones on the ward." Francesca laughed at the man's statement, for she knew he couldn't be referring to her. "So how are you getting on?" he asked. "I

understand you're waiting for your final results. No wonder you were left in charge last night. Sister must rate you highly, to give you that amount of responsibility."

"I'm doing well, thank you." she said, "and I was only in charge last night, because one of the staff nurses was off sick, and Sister couldn't rearrange the off duty to have one of the others on duty, so I did a split duty. And then the girl who was going to be in charge was taken away by one of the other wards who didn't have any staff at all."

"Complicated" he said with a smile. "So where are you off to now?"

"I'm going back to the ward" she replied. "I had to go and see the nursing officer about something that happened last night- she needed to know the full details, and while I was there, she told me that if I pass my exams, then I've got the job I wanted."

"Congratulations" he said "where do you want to work?"

"Theatres" she answered him with a smile. "I really loved my time there when I did my placement, and the Sister told me I'd be most welcome if I wanted to go back. Don't get me wrong, I like being able to talk to my patients when they're awake, but I like the idea of working in theatres."

"Well, good for you" he said. "I hope you'll be very happy."

"Thank you" she said, and then "I'd better go. I might see you on the ward, but in the meantime, please give your father my best wishes."

"I will do" he nodded, and she went on her way. He appeared to be very friendly, and she felt at ease with him. She smiled to herself, and ran up the stairs to the ward. When she got back, Sister and Staff Nurse were in the office, but they waved to show that they had seen her, and she went to the table to talk to Ally, who was busy totting up some fluid balance charts. "Everything okay?" she was asked, and she nodded. "I had to go and see Miss Lines about what happened last night" she said. "But before I came back, she told me that if I do pass the exams, then I've got a job in theatres if I want it. She said she'll be talking to all our set to let them know what jobs they can expect to get if they pass. So, you might be lucky enough to be able to stay here." she grinned delightedly at her friend. "Good" Ally said, then looked at her watch. "I think I'd better go to tea, then when I come back, you'll be able to go home. I'll just let Sister know where I'm going, and take the auxiliary with me. We're going to be short of staff again tonight. Let's hope nothing happens like it did last night."

"No," agreed Francesca. "But I've just seen Mr. Daniels son, and he said his father is doing very well, and will hopefully be coming back to us, probably tomorrow."

"His son?" queried Ally, "I didn't think he'd got a son. His daughter is the only person who's visited him, since he was admitted.

"Well, the guy who visited last night, said he was visiting his father, and I've just seen him again, and when I asked how Mr. Daniels was doing, he said his father was doing well." She laughed "We can't very well ask for identification, can we? If he says he's his father, then we have to believe him."

“You're right” Ally agreed, and stood up. “Add these balance charts up for me, will you? You were always better at maths than I am.”
“Well, an A level in Maths does come in handy sometimes.” Francesca laughed. “Go on, go and have your tea, and then I can go home.” and she watched as her friend went on her way. Left alone, she added up the fluid balance sheets, and took them back to the patients they belonged to, tidying up the lockers as she went, and making sure that nobody wanted anything special. Ally still wasn't back, when Sister came into the ward. “Fran, go off duty” she said. “You worked late yesterday, didn't have any breaks, and you're owed quite a bit of time anyway. I'm here and so is Staff Nurse Davies, so we can look after the ward.”
“Thanks Sister.” Francesca smiled at her. She said her goodbyes and walked away from the ward, slowly, because there was nothing for her to look forward to, when she was off duty,
and she had reached the intersection of the corridors, when she saw Mr. Daniels son standing by the wall. “I'm glad I didn't miss you” he said, to surprise her. “I wondered if you fancied going out for a drink with me? It would be nice to have somebody to talk to who could tell me what's been happening, but I promise not to talk about your work all the time.” Francesca gaped at him. She'd only met him on a couple of occasions, but he appeared quite nice, and she knew very little about him, but she had liked him immediately, and felt at ease with him, and she needn't see him again if she didn't want to. She made up her mind, and nodded. “Okay” she

said, “that would be nice. Where do you want me to meet you, and at what time?”
“How about going to the Feathers?” he asked. “It's quite a nice pub, or so I've been told, but not a lot of hospital people go there. I could meet you inside about 7.30 if that would be acceptable?”
“Sounds okay to me” she agreed, and wondered as she went on her way after saying a temporary farewell, why he had asked her. She was still wondering, when her sister phoned to ask her how she was. “I'm okay” she said, “We had a bit of a problem last night, one of our patients arrested, and our student nurse didn't, or couldn't do a thing. When we'd got rid of the patient to ITU and looked for her, she'd disappeared. I had to go and see Miss Lines this afternoon, and explain everything to her. She told me that if I pass my exams, theatres want me to go back.”
“Oh, Fran, that's wonderful. I know you always liked it there. You'll be very happy to be going back to somewhere you enjoyed so much. But what happened with the student nurse?”
Francesca explained that the girl would not be returning to the hospital, and Samantha laughed.
“What I wondered was if you wanted to come and have a drink or a meal with me tonight? We could have a chat about whether you wanted to have a look for a flat near here, or whether you wanted to stay in the nurses home?”
“No, I haven't made a decision yet” Francesca insisted, “but I can't come tonight. I've been invited for a drink with somebody”
“Who?” her sister asked, and Francesca had to tell

her. “He's the son of one of my patients, and it was his father who arrested last night. He seems to be quite nice, and just invited me for a drink to say thanks for all the hard work we did. So, I said I'd meet him this evening.”

“Where are you going?” was the question, but somehow Francesca didn't want her sister to know. She wanted to be able to keep him a secret for a while. “Oh, just to a pub nearby” she said. “Sam, I've got to get something to eat before I go out, so I'd better go.”

“Well, you take care. Make sure he doesn't take advantage of you.” was her sisters’ advice. “Enjoy yourself and let me know how you get on.”

“I will” Francesca said, and replaced the receiver after saying her farewells. Her sister had carried on her mother's work, looking after her, treating her like a little girl, which she sometimes resented, and she wondered if Sam realised her sister was an adult now, with a career of her own. She thought not, then shrugged. Sometimes it was nice to be looked after, but not always. She hurried off to the kitchen where she made herself a sandwich, which she took back to her room to eat, and then went into the bathroom, where she had a swift bath and washed her hair, before dressing hurriedly. She had pulled on a blue dress, which fitted snugly and had short sleeves and she had always liked it. It wasn't new, but it was one of the last dresses she had bought when her mother had been alive, and in fact her mother had pointed it out to her, as it hung on the rail when they had been shopping together. It had not looked anything on the rail, but on Francesca's

figure, it looked stunning. She wore sandals on her feet, and looked cool, because the day had been very warm. She had allowed her hair to flow down her back, drawn back from her face with a bandeau, and hadn't applied much make up.
She hesitated before going downstairs, wondering if she was doing the right thing, for she didn't go into pubs very often, for she had had to look after her mother in her final illness, while she was younger, and she hadn't been out very often when she started her training, for she had lived at home, and not in the nurses home. Her sister was a different kettle of fish, having had lots of friends while she was training, going out with them on many occasions, and being a much more sociable type of person, whereas Francesca was more introverted. She sighed, and caught up her handbag. She had promised to go for a drink with the man, and she knew she would be able to leave fairly early, if she didn't want to stay. She made sure she had her keys, shut the door behind her, and ran downstairs.

The Feathers pub was situated a few streets away, nearer to her old home, than the hospital, but she knew the streets nearby, very well, and didn't worry about walking around them. When she reached the door, she hesitated, then took a deep breath, and walked inside and glanced around her. Mr. Cavanagh was waiting for her, and came to greet her. She smiled at him, and said hello before he escorted her to a table nearby. “Hello” he said now. “I was hoping you wouldn't decide to stand me up.” he grinned at her. “How come you have one

surname and your father has a different one?" she said, before she could stop herself. Dominic smiled at her puzzlement. "He's actually my stepfather," he said, "which explains it. He married my mother after my own father passed away, and bought me up, so I think of him as my father." he sighed, "Now, what can I get you to drink?"
"Could I have a glass of white wine, please?" she asked, and he nodded. "Won't be a minute" he said, and walked across to the bar. He was soon back, bearing the drinks, and he placed her glass in front of her, as he took his seat opposite her. "How's your father now?" she asked after she took a sip of the drink, and he grinned. "He's doing very well. He's going to be transferred back to your ward tomorrow morning, and I don't think he can wait to get back to it. I know he feels a lot better than he did. He'll obviously be in a lot longer than he had wanted to stay, but he realises that this latest problem is going to extend his stay." He took a drink, then sat back against the seat and looked at her. "That's a very pretty dress" he remarked, "you look very cool, calm and collected. Are you like that when you're working when there isn't an emergency?"
"Thank you" she replied, "I hope I'm able to keep my head if there's a problem."
"I've been told you are waiting for your results. When are they due out?"
"Five weeks' time" she said. "We're all on edge waiting for them. We took our exams three weeks ago, and we don't get the results for eight weeks, so you can imagine that we're all a bit short tempered these days." He laughed and nodded. She thought

back to the remarks Ally had made and said, “Mr. Daniels only appeared to have a daughter to visit when he was first admitted. Have you been away?”
“Yes” he nodded, “I was abroad working, and didn't come back permanently until a few weeks ago. I stayed with him when I got back but I'd gone away again, visiting some friends in the north of the country for few weeks, got back a couple of days ago, phoned Dad, and got told` that he was in hospital. I visited last night, and of course he'd just had the arrest, so I didn't get to have a long chat with him, as they'd hooked him up to loads of machines on ITU.”
“What about your mother?” she asked, “Is she able to visit him?” he shook his head, “No, Mum died two years ago, and after that Dad didn't really want to carry on. I was abroad, as I said, but I kept in touch with phone calls and video calls, but he was very downhearted. It's taken all this time to get him to enjoy living again. I was hoping that when I got back to England, we'd be able to get together properly, and spend a lot more time together, but things haven't worked out too well, so far anyway. My stepsister looked after him while I was away and he appreciated it.”
“He's such a nice man” Francesca smiled at the memory. “He never seemed to be very downhearted, even after the operation, and he was doing so well. He'd been out of bed and gone for a short walk with the physio's yesterday morning as well.”
“That's what he told me this morning.” Dominic agreed, then changed the subject. “What about you?

Do you have any family living nearby, or are they all miles away from here?"
"My sister lives in a flat near the hospital, and my brother and his wife have a house about five miles away. Sam, my sister is a Senior staff nurse on the medical unit, is very intent on her career, and has no interest in getting married, and my brother is a junior registrar on the Orthopaedic Unit. They're a lot older than I am, I was the afterthought of the family. My father died about fifteen years ago – he was a consultant surgeon at the hospital, and my mother died nearly a year ago. We lived in a large house about a mile away from here, but that's been sold now, and I finally moved out completely about three days ago."
"Oh, I'm sorry" he said. "I know how horrible it is, when you lose a close relative. But at least you had your job to keep you occupied."
"No, I didn't" she disagreed. "Mum became terminally ill about fifteen months before she died, and I stopped my training to look after her. Miss Lines, the nursing office, agreed that I could have a break, and come back to it, when the end finally happened. I started my training nearly five years ago, but I'm only just coming to the end of it now." she stopped, and took a drink, aware that she wanted to cry, and not wanting to do so in front of this man. She felt at home with him, and knew that if she hadn't done so, she would never have told him what she had just done. She took a deep breath, and smiled tremulously at him. "Mum and I were very good friends as well as being mother and daughter. I think it was because I was the youngest, so when she

became so ill, I knew I wanted to spend as much time as I possibly could with her. I think I managed to give her some enjoyment in her final months. I'd take her out shopping, we went to see her friends and I nursed her until the end. And then I stayed, living in the house, but working at the hospital, until my brother and sister wanted it to be sold, and I had to move out."

"So, you live in the nurses home now?" he asked gently, and she nodded. "Sam wants me to find myself a flat, but I'm not going to bother, until I make up my mind about whether I want to stay here, or move away. I've lived in this area all my life, so I know it very well, but I wonder whether I ought to move and get some experience of another part of the world. I don't want to have the bother of having to sell a flat and move again, until I've decided what to do." He patted her hand in silent sympathy, and she smiled as she looked at him. "Sorry" she said, "I didn't mean to tell you everything like that. I think I needed to talk to somebody, and I'm afraid you got the short straw." He laughed at her expression, "Don't worry" he said. "I think you needed to get it all off your chest as it were. So how old are you, if you don't mind me asking?"

"I'm nearly 25." she replied. "I hadn't started training until I was nearly 20. I'd been helping Mum with her work, but I'd always wanted to be a nurse, and when Mum got her book published, she decided she didn't need me to stay at home anymore, so I applied to train."

"Her book?" he asked and she nodded. "Mum was a historian, and she wrote a book about Lady Jane

Grey. It's now acknowledged as the stand out work on the woman, and I helped her with her research. It was fascinating, and Mum really enjoyed writing it. I'm glad she saw its publication and the good reviews on it, before she passed away."

"So you come from a very educated family – your siblings are in the medical profession, as was your father, and your mother was a historian." She nodded, then said, "but they're much cleverer than I am. I just like looking after people." she hesitated, then, "What about you? You said you were working abroad. What did you do and what country were you working in?"

"Oh, I was doing research and teaching in New Zealand. I loved it – it's a beautiful country and I thoroughly enjoyed exploring it when I had time to do so." He told her of some of the places he had seen, and she was entranced by his description of the country, for he was enlarging on some of the places he had visited, when one of her acquaintances, came across to them, and said "Hi Fran. Nice to see you again." She looked up, and saw Janet, a girl who she had trained with when she had first started, and who was now working as a staff nurse on one of the surgical wards, and smiled up at her. "Hi Janet." she said. "How are you doing? Okay?" and the other girl nodded and looked vaguely startled when she saw who Francesca was with. "Sorry I disturbed you" she said, "I'll leave you to it" she said, "Bye" and she walked away, with her companions. "I started training with Janet, when I started, the first time." she explained, "but she's now qualified. But I liked hearing about your trip. It sounds lovely. I might

think about working there, if I do decide to go away from here."
"Do a lot of research before you decide what you want to do" he advised her. "I spent a lot of time making my mind up, when I had the chance to go abroad, and I'm glad I was able to go somewhere I was very happy, but it's a very long way away, right away from all your friends and relatives, and you wouldn't know anybody there, if you do decide to go." He grinned suddenly, and looked years younger. "This sounds like a careers advisory service lecture" he said, and they both smiled. "Don't worry, I'd talk everything over with the family first" she said, "and of course, I've got to pass my exams before anything can happen. I will need to get at least one years' experience as well, so I've got a long time before I can make up my mind to do something different." He grinned at her again, and changed the subject. She realised that she was able to talk to him, about a lot of different things, and heard with a sense of shock, the call for last orders. "We've been in here hours" she said, and smiled. "But I'm glad I came. Thank you for inviting me."
"Think nothing of it" he said. "Do you fancy coming out again sometime?" She nodded, and they made a date for the following weekend. "I'm on an early Saturday and a late duty on Sunday" she said, and he grinned. "I'll be starting work in the next few weeks, so I won't have much spare time after that, but I'm sure we can fit in time for a drink or something, but only if you want to."
"I did enjoy myself tonight" she said, and he grinned at her. "I'll see you home" he said, as they left the

pub, but she shook her head. “I only live in the nurses home, and I've known this area for a long time” she protested, but he was adamant, and accompanied her back to the gates of the hospital. “Thanks” she said, “Goodnight” and she would have turned away to go into the nurses home, but he took her hand, bent and kissed her on the cheek. “Goodnight Francesca.” he said quietly. Sleep well.” and watched as she walked swiftly to the nurses home, before turning away to walk home.

Chapter Three

"Well?" queried Ally when the two girls met at breakfast time the following day. "Where did you go, what's his name and what did you talk about?" She grinned at her friend, as they prepared themselves a meal in the small kitchen. "His name's Dominic, we went to a pub, and we just talked." Francesca said. "He's Mr. Daniels stepson, not his son, and he told me about New Zealand, he's been working there, teaching and doing research.
"Are you going out with him again?" Ally asked and Francesca nodded. "We're going out for dinner tomorrow evening. I'm on an early, so I should be off duty in time. We just seemed to get on very well together."
"Good for you" Ally said, as they went back to Francesca's room to eat their small meal. "You need some fun, after what you've been through."
"Was everything alright on the ward yesterday evening?" Francesca asked, and Ally nodded. "Mr. Daniels is coming back today" she said, "providing all the tests are good, but I think he's going to need a special nurse for a day or so."
"Makes sense, I suppose" Francesca agreed, and still talking about their patients, the two girls made their way to the ward. The day went ahead, Mr. Daniels was returned to the ward, and Francesca was detailed to keep a very close eye on the man. The old man seemed to be in very good spirits, and told her he was delighted to be back on the ward again. "Not that they weren't good to me in the Unit" he said, "they were, but they weren't the nurses I've got to

know. And my stepson came to see me" he said, smiling at her, "he's been working away for a long time, but he's been back in the country now for a couple of months, and he's able to see me again. He's been busy buying himself somewhere to live, because he's going to settle down now, or so he maintains." the old man said dryly, and Francesca grinned at him.
"I talked to him and he was very pleased to be able to see you again." she agreed, and the old man sighed. "He's a good boy, and very clever" he said. "He's got a new job as well, so I don't suppose I'll see as much of him as I would like, but I'm glad he's in this country and not so far away as he was." Francesca agreed with him, not revealing that she had been given details of his stepson's previous job, and asked if he would be visiting that day. "Well, he said he hoped he would be able to come and see me this evening. My daughter will be visiting this afternoon, if she can, but she's got the children to look after, so it's a bit difficult."
"How many grandchildren do you have?" she asked, and the old man smiled as he replied "Four. They're thirteen, ten, seven and the youngest is just three years old, and a handful, I can tell you. I live quite separately, in an annexe in my daughter's house, and the children come and see me very frequently. In fact, it was my eldest grandson, who found me, when I fell and had the accident. He's a good lad, he wants to be a doctor when he grows up. I tell him he's got to study hard and pass his exams, and he's very good, but I don't know whether he'll change his mind as he gets older."

"Well, you just lie back, and have a nap, and you'll be rested when she comes to visit you." Francesca advised, and the old man laid back against the pillows, and did as he was told, after telling her she was a bully. Francesca made sure that he was doing well, and thought with regret, that she wouldn't see his stepson that afternoon. She would have to wait until the following afternoon, she thought to herself, and knew she was looking forward to her evening out. When she got off duty that afternoon, she phoned her sister, only to find that she was unavailable, so left a message on the answerphone, telling Sam that she wouldn't be in the following evening, and she would contact her, when she was able to. Ally was going out that evening with her fiancée, so she wasn't going to be available, so Francesca made herself a cup of tea, and took it, and her washing kit, to the bathroom, where she ran herself a hot bath, and lay in it for a long time, just thinking about her old home. Eventually, she got out, and dried herself, and went back to her room, and laid on the bed, put the radio on, and relaxed against the pillows, reading one of the books she had bought with her from her old home. She realised she wasn't taking in anything she read, and put down the book, as she thought more about her home. She remembered the way she had felt after her father died, and how her mother had looked after her. She had been nine when he passed away, and she only had a child's memory of him, but her mother had told her so many things about him, and his work. He had been an orthopaedic surgeon, and her brother had followed his example, specialising in that branch of medicine after he had qualified. She had seen her brother that morning, when he came to do a round, but they hadn't spoken about anything apart from the patients, and in fact, he hadn't spoken to her very often, since the house had been sold. She wondered whether he felt any remorse about the fact that he and Theresa had insisted that the house should be sold, but doubted it. She had known herself that it wasn't practical for her to remain in the house on her own, for it was a large house, and cost a lot to maintain, but it had been her home, and she had lots of memories and been happy there. She sighed, turned the radio off, put out the lights and was soon asleep.

Several of her friends had been told where they would be working if they passed their exams, and the ones who were staying at the hospital had been glad to hear the news. They were having coffee that morning, and discussing what they were going to do after their results came out. "We are going to have a party aren't we If we pass?" Eloise asked, another of the group, and there were murmurs of agreement. "Why don't we discuss it tonight?" she said. "I'm not going out, what about the rest of you?"
"Sorry, count me out" Francesca said, "I'm going out to dinner, but make your arrangements and I'll fit in with your plans." Thankfully nobody asked who she was going out to dinner with, for she didn't really want to tell anybody about him. As it was, her friends thought she would be dining with her sister, for she had frequently done so, since she had moved into the nurses home. Now she looked at her watch.

“I've got to go back girls. See you” she said, and stood up. Her departure started a general exodus, and they sped back to their respective wards.

She had got off duty on time, and gone to her room to get ready for the evening, wondering what she wear, for her wardrobe wasn’t that extensive. She dressed, eventually, in a short sleeve dress, in a chestnut colour with darker bands of colour around the sleeves and the hem, pulled her hair back and caught up her coat and handbag, and walked downstairs to the entrance, where they had agreed to meet.

Dominic was waiting for her when she arrived, and smiled broadly, when he saw her approach. “The car's over here” he said, and led her to the car park, where he opened the door of a dark blue Bentley Arnage. She looked at it, and her eyes opened wide. “What a fantastic car” she finally said, and he grinned. “I bought it when I got back to England” he said, “I'd been intending to buy one and I found this one really quickly. What with buying a house and buying the car as well, it’s been a busy and expensive couple of months.” he shut the door behind her, and she sat back in the leather seat. He started the engine, and pulled out into the traffic outside the hospital, before heading out of the city, and into the country beyond. The drive to the restaurant took a while, and she was wondering where they were going when he pulled up outside a restaurant, several miles away from the hospital, and came round to open the door for her. She looked up at the building and realised it was very old. "Don't worry," he said quietly, "it's been modernised. I've been here before, and I think you might like it." He took her arm, and led her into the restaurant, and they were escorted to their table, by a waiter, who produced menus and a wine list, and took her coat. Francesca looked around her, wondering whether her dress was suitable for the restaurant, but Dominic smiled at her. "You look nice" he said "and that dress really suits you. I liked the one you wore on Thursday as well." She looked down at the menu, as she thanked him, not accustomed to receiving compliments on her dress sense. They exchanged smiles, and she looked again at the menu. "I have absolutely no idea what to pick to eat" she said and he smiled. "The menu is very extensive, isn't it?" he said. "But what would you like to drink first?" She chose white wine, but Dominic chose a non-alcoholic drink, "I'm driving" he said as she looked surprised, and she nodded her understanding. The wine, when it arrived, was superb, and she knew it was a very expensive one. "Is it okay?" he asked, and she nodded again. "It's gorgeous, like drinking silk if you know what I mean," she said, and he grinned. "It's one of my favourites" he said. "I found the vineyard when I was in New Zealand, and tasted it, and since then, I very rarely drink any other white, if I have a choice. I'm lucky they export it to the United Kingdom, otherwise if I really wanted it, I'd have to import it for myself. Now, what shall we have to eat?" and they discussed their choices. Their order given, he asked her what her off duty for the following week was, and nodded at her answer. “I shall be free on Tuesday and Thursday” he said. “Would you like to come and have a drink again with me on Tuesday? Or, we could go out for another meal, if you like? And as you're free on Thursday afternoon, perhaps we could drive down to the coast, and go for a walk, and then out to dinner afterwards, if you'd like that.” She nodded, aware that she liked him very much and wanted to spend more time with him. They sat for a long time, over their meal, just talking about their likes and dislikes, and although she had resolved not to tell him anything too deep about herself, she found herself telling him of things that had happened in her childhood. He had asked about her parents, and she wanted to tell him about them. “My father died when I was nine” she said, “and I thought he was quite young when he passed away, but now I know he was a lot older than mum, and he was approaching retirement age when he died. I was the afterthought of the family. My brother qualified about two years after Dad died, and now he's a registrar, and he's specialising in Orthopaedics. He's meant to be quite good, but I've never worked with him, until this placement, and I have no idea what he's like in theatre. His wife has just told us that she's expecting a baby in about five months’ time, so I'll soon be an aunty, and Andy will be busy with work, and a new baby!” she grinned at Dominic. “He's got a new boss, who's starting work soon, so I hope he gets on well with the man. Everybody's been wondering what the new man’s like, but he's arrived now, so he'll be starting soon, and they'll find out. Ally and I were wondering whether or not he'd

be okay towards the student nurses, and not find them a total pain, like some of the other surgeons do."
"Are there surgeons who don't like student nurses then?" he asked, and she nodded. "There are at least two general surgeons and one Orthopaedic man, who don't like student nurses. I was told by one, when I was a first-year student, that we are a complete nuisance, and he was sorry he'd ever come to work at a teaching hospital. He left about a year later, and we heard he'd gone to work in a private hospital that never has student nurses. Most of the surgeons are quite nice though, and teach us girls as much as they can."
"I would have thought it was better for the nurses to be taught everything they know, so they can look after the patients to the surgeon's satisfaction."
"Yes," she agreed, "we know that, but there are some who can't seem to get that concept into their heads. I do hope this new man isn't going to be one of them."
"Haven't you met him then?" Dominic asked, and she shook her head. "He was bought round by Miss Lines, and introduced to some of the senior staff, but as a student, I wasn't worthy of an introduction, so I just got on with doing the dressings, and when I'd finished, he'd gone. I expect I'll meet him sometime," she laughed.
"You were saying that you're going to be an aunty. You didn't sound very impressed. Don't you like children?"
"I do like them," she said, "but I've not had much to do with them. What about you? Your father told me

you've got nephews and nieces. Do you get on with them?"
"Yes, we get on quite well, and I'd quite like to have some of my own one day" he grinned at her. "My oldest nephew has decided he wants to be a doctor, and my father is encouraging him. He" he stopped suddenly, and changed the subject. "What are your sister and brother called. You said your brother is Andy?" She nodded. "Yes, he's Andrew, but known as Andy, and my sister is Samantha, but known universally as Sam. My mother always called me Francesca, but everybody in the hospital calls me Fran, so we're Fran, Sam and Andy." She smiled at him. "Were you ever called Dom?" she asked, and he nodded. "However, I managed to nip that in the bud, so it's always Dominic now. I hate contractions of names, so I'll call you Francesca, it's a lovely name, and shouldn't be shortened." he smiled at her, as he took her hand across the table. "It's a lovely name, for a lovely girl" he said softly, and she felt herself blush. "Thank you" she whispered, and he laughed. "Hasn't anybody called you lovely before, because you are, you know?" She shook her head. "I don't think I am" she said, "my mother always called me homely. I don't go out very often anyway" she said quietly. "Sam and Andy didn't live at home, I didn't have many friends when I was acting as Mum's researcher, because all the people I'd gone to school with, had left to go to University, and when I started nursing, I had to study hard, because I was older than most of the girls." She looked at him, and was surprised to see an expression of puzzlement on his face. "Didn't you want to go to University?" he

asked, and she nodded. “I was going to read History or Maths, before I started to train as a nurse, but then Mum found out I was good at research, and she asked me if I'd be able to help, and after that, my dreams of university went out of the window. After we'd finished the book, I did think about it again, but then decided I'd forget about university and be a nurse instead.”

“But you must have had a few A levels to even think about going to University” he said, and she nodded.

“I've got four – Pure and Applied Maths, History and English Language” she said, and grinned at the look on his face. “And you said your family were cleverer than you? I don't think so, Francesca. To get that lot, you must have had to work hard. They're such disparate subjects apart from the two Maths ones of course.”

“I did my English Language earlier than the other three,” she confessed. “I thoroughly enjoyed doing that, and then did the others in the Upper sixth form. I liked school as you can imagine.”

“Obviously.” he said dryly. “Perhaps you would like to talk to my niece and nephew and tell them that if they work hard, they could do as well as you could.”

She looked down at the tablecloth, for his words had implied that he wanted the relationship to continue, and she didn't know how to respond to his statement. “Poor Francesca” he said softly, continuing to hold her hand. “I shouldn't make statements like that, until we get to know each other a lot better, should I? I'm sorry.” He looked at his watch – a very thin gold one, with a gold-coloured strap. “I think we'd better be going. It's getting

quite late, and you've got to work tomorrow. What time will you finish tomorrow evening?"
"Nine thirty" she admitted, as he beckoned the waiter and asked for the bill. "There's not a chance to do anything after we come off duty, but I don't mind. The hospital management are considering going over to a two-shift system – 12 hours each day, and night, because they say it would be better for us, because we'd have four days off together, occasionally, instead of two, but at the moment we all like the three-shift system. But it's not up to us. We just do what they tell us to do." The waiter had taken the credit card payment for the bill, and bought her, her coat, and Dominic held it for her to put on. They went out to the car, and she was struck anew by his good manners as he opened the door for her. He took her home, a different way, going through small villages that were quiet, and the side roads were unfamiliar to her. At last, they reached the outskirts of the city, and he pulled into the side of the road. "I would suggest taking you to my new house for a final drink, but it's being redecorated and it's in a bit of a muddle," he said, "so if you don't mind, I think I'll say goodnight to you here, and not outside the hospital, under the gaze of anybody who has the time to spare to look out of the window" and he bent his head, and kissed her. She had been kissed before, occasionally, but this kiss was nothing like that, and she knew she liked it. He lifted his head, stared into her eyes, before he kissed her again, and this time, she kissed him back. "Oh Francesca" he said, as he lifted his head, then she saw him smile in the light from a nearby street lamp.

"I hope you didn't mind" he said softly, and she shook her head. "No, not at all." she whispered, and he smiled again, as he bent his head again. He was holding her close, his hands rubbing her back, as his mouth explored hers, and when he lifted his head, she was breathless. "I thought perhaps you were having second thoughts, when we were talking just now," she said softly, "but that proves you weren't. I'm sorry for doubting you." and he kissed her again. "I'm looking forward to Tuesday already" he murmured, and smiled at her. "But now, I think I'd better take you back to the nurses home." He kissed her again, then put her away from him, and started the engine of the car again. When he drove into the car park, he kissed her on the cheek. "Goodnight Francesca" he said softly, as she got out, "See you on Tuesday" and watched as she ran across the forecourt, and into the nurses home.

She reached her room, and closed the door behind her, turning on the bedside lamp, as she pulled the curtains. She had thoroughly enjoyed her evening with Dominic, and the end of the evening had been the most enjoyable part. She opened her handbag and took out her phone, which was also her alarm clock, and saw she had missed a call from her sister, and listened to the voicemail message. Her sister hoped she was enjoying her evening, and told her that she would contact her soon. Francesca prepared for bed as if in a dream, and as she turned off the light, she knew she would sleep well.

Since that evening, she had been out with

Dominic several times in the following four weeks, before he started his new job, spending time with him, either in a pub having a drink or going to restaurants. His father had been discharged, nearly three weeks after his emergency, and Dominic had told her that he was doing very well, and she was glad to hear it, because she had liked the old man. He had said one day, when they had been walking along the path by a canal, that his stepfather had wondered how she was getting on. "I almost told him" Dominic grinned at her, "but I didn't want to tell him that I was still seeing you. I'm not ashamed of you, don't think that, but if I'd said that I was going out with you, he and Elizabeth, my stepsister would have wanted to know all about you, and I want to keep you to myself for a bit, if you don't mind."
"I don't mind at all" Francesca admitted. "I haven't told anybody about you either. Samantha knows that I'm going out with somebody, who is the son of one of my patients, but I've never told her your name." Dominic grinned at her, as he took her hand, then caught her to him and kissed her. "I'm glad we feel the same way" he said. "You must be wondering why I've never taken you to my house, but it's still being redecorated at the moment, and it's a bit of a mess, but I promise I'll take you there one day."
"I did wonder where you lived" she admitted, "but I hadn't been too concerned."
"Good" he admitted, "the decorators should be finished very soon, so I'll take you and show you round. The house hadn't been decorated for quite a

while, when I first bought it, and it was very old fashioned, so it needed to be smartened up a bit. It's been fun choosing colours, but perhaps I shouldn't have chosen them myself. Perhaps I should have waited, and asked somebody" and he grinned at her, before kissing her again. She didn't say anything, couldn't say a word, and he laughed at her expression, before releasing her, and walking on. She followed him, wondering if he did mean what he said, but decided not to say anything. They walked slowly back towards the hospital, to collect the car, before going out for a meal that evening to a restaurant that was very exclusive. At the end of the evening, Dominic dropped her off outside the hospital, and she walked into the building, knowing that she felt extremely happy when she was with him, and as she opened the door of her room, realised that she was in love with him, wanted to spend more time with him, and never leave him again. She didn't know how to deal with her feelings, but her dreams that night were full of Dominic, and the way he made her feel.

When she went on duty the following day, she was puzzled by the attitude of the staff nurse she had been working with, the day before. Whereas, she had always been treated with consideration by the senior staff, today, the staff nurse didn't tell her to get on with things, she suggested it instead, and the change seemed odd. In the end, she asked her what the problem was, but the answer puzzled her even more. "Well, we've got to make sure you're happy" as the answer, and Francesca walked away,

wondering what to do. She forgot about it, as she went about her business, greeting the visitors, and talking to them, before getting on with the business of looking after the patients. She went off duty that evening, tired after her days work, and got back to her room. She was making herself a drink, when Ally came knocking at the door, holding out a mug of tea.
“I'd just made one” she said, “and I heard you come in, so thought you might like it.”
“You're a life saver” Francesca said, with a smile. “Supper was a hurried affair, because we had an admission, and I got called back to deal with it. He was being taken to theatre this evening, so we were busy getting everything ready.” The two girls discussed the admission for a while, until Ally suddenly asked, “Fran, who did you go out with last night?”
“Mr. Daniels stepson. His name is Dominic, but I told you that when I'd gone out for a drink with him after the first time, I'd been with him. I've been out with him several times since then. Why are you asking?”
“Well, there are some very odd rumours flying around” Ally confessed, and Francesca looked at her friend. “What about?” she asked, and was extremely surprised when Ally said simply “You.”
“Me?” Francesca said. “What am I meant to have done?”
“I don't know” Ally said simply. “I heard people in the canteen talking about you, they were mentioning your name, but when I walked nearer, they stopped, and started talking about other things. I reckon they knew that I am your best friend. But, honest Fran, it was really odd, I can tell you.”

"Well, I don't think I've done anything." she said. "I went out with Dominic last night, we got back here about midnight, said goodnight, and I came back here to bed. I haven't had a chance to do anything." She grinned at her friend, "I'd love to know what I'm meant to have done. If you get a chance to find out, please do tell me, because I'm intrigued now."
"Okay, I'll keep my ears open, and try and find out" Ally said, then "Did you enjoy yourself last night anyway, and where did you go?"
"I had a lovely time thank you, and we went to a hotel that had a restaurant attached. It was called The Hayrack and it was miles away from here."
"It's got a good reputation" she said. "I've heard of it, but I've never met anybody who's been there. Is it expensive?"
"I think so." she admitted. "But it was very nice"
"What did you eat and drink?" she was asked, and when Francesca told her, her eyes opened wide.
"That sounds a lot better than the burger and chips that Simon bought me after we'd been to the cinema." she admitted. "He bought a couple of tins of drink as well, but your wine sounds gorgeous."
"It was" she said with a smile as she remembered the drink. "It was like drinking silk, if you know what I mean. It just slipped down the throat, and he said that he'd first found it when he was in New Zealand, and thought it was lucky that they exported it to this country, otherwise he said he'd have had to imported it himself. It's the one he always buys for me, when we go out." She grinned at her friend, "I thought he was joking about importing it, but now I'm not too certain about that" she said. "But that

cup of tea was just what I needed to relax with after a long and busy day at work. Thanks Ally". Francesca yawned, and Ally grinned at her in sympathy. "I'll let you go and get some sleep. After an evening like today, I think you probably need it. But you've got to answer one more question" she said, and Francesca wondered what she was going to say. "Is he serious?" she was asked, but Francesca didn't answer straight away. "I don't know" she admitted. "I like him very much, he makes me feel good, but whether or not he's serious, I haven't got any idea. But I am going to go to bed now, I'm really tired. Night Ally." The other girl smiled as she picked up the mug and went to the door. "Sleep well" she was told, as she left the room, and by the time Francesca was ready for bed, and had set her alarm clock for the next morning, she was too tired to think about reading her book, and after turning the light out, she was soon asleep.

The following morning, she went on duty to find that one of the staff nurses hadn't come on duty, so they were very short staffed again, especially as Celia hadn't been replaced, so she was very busy. Luckily, the senior staff nurse was in charge, and she was able to continue with her work in peace. She had gone to the canteen at lunchtime to have a small meal, and was sitting with some of her friends, when Janet came up to her table. "You didn't waste much time, did you?" was the comment. "You'll have to teach me your tricks" she said, then walked away. Francesca looked after her, then at her friends. "What on earth was that all about?" she asked, but they had no idea, and the talk turned back to generalities.

Chapter Four

It was a week away from when she would be getting her results, when she went onto the ward on Monday morning, Francesca sensed that there was a different atmosphere on the ward. It was busy, as per usual and she was kept occupied, looking after the patients, until Sister came to talk to her. "Fran, I'm sorry to ask this, but I wondered if you'd be able to go and take charge on Exeter Ward just for the rest of the day? Miss Lines has just phoned, and asked if that would be okay. She said that as you're nearly qualified, you would be the ideal person to help. The sister on the ward has just had to go off duty because she's not well, and there aren't any other senior staff on duty. If you wouldn't mind going now, you'd be helping her." Francesca nodded – it wasn't unheard of for senior students to have to go and help on other wards. "Am I to stay all day?" she asked and Sister nodded. "Please" she said, "but you'll be back here tomorrow. Miss Lines will be contacting some of the staff who are off duty, and asking them to come in tomorrow." She didn't like Exeter Ward very much, it was a medical ward, and she hadn't much enjoyed her stint working there when she was a junior student, but went to the cloakroom to gather together her cloak and the bag, that she had taken on duty that morning, and after waving farewell to her patients, she left the ward and made her way to Exeter Ward. When she arrived, the ward was in chaos – there were only junior students on duty, and it was obvious they didn't have very much idea of what was happening, and a consultant round due to take place in a very short time. She hurriedly read the report, gained an idea of what was going on, and allocated the nurses to look after the patients. She had hurriedly gathered the notes and x rays together, and just in time, for the consultant and his team arrived for the round. The round took a very long time, and by the time it was finished, she was exhausted. The consultant was known for his attention to detail, and it had taken a long time for him to give his orders relating to the patients. He had been kind to her, taking into account her lack of information about the patients, but all the same, she felt that the patients needed a permanent senior nurse, and hoped that the Sister or staff nurse would be back soon. She had dealt with lunches, but hadn't been able to leave the ward, when the late staff came on duty, because there was nobody senior enough to take over, so she had eaten a sandwich in the kitchen, and drunk a cup of tea made especially for her by the ward maid. She was writing the report on the patients later that afternoon, when her sister phoned the ward, to speak to the absent ward Sister. "Fran, is that you?" she said when she heard her sister's voice. "What are you doing on Exeter Ward?" Francesca laughed, "Sister Dempster went off sick, both staff nurses are also off sick, or on days off, and there wasn't anybody who was able to take charge of the ward, so Miss Lines asked Sister Eames if I could come and take over for the day. I hope she's found somebody to take over this evening, because I don't particularly want to stay on duty for 13 hours. She hasn't phoned yet, so I'm still waiting to hear." Her

sister sympathised with her. "I'm sure you won't have to." she said quietly, "in fact, I know you won't have to. We've got one of the other staff nurses on with me, so if I borrow one of the juniors from your ward, then we could do a swap. I'll phone her and offer in a minute. All I wanted to know was if you could lend me some Methylated Spirits? We ran out yesterday apparently, and when I went to get some this afternoon, of course, everybody had forgotten to order it. The pharmacy doesn't have any until tomorrow morning."
"I'm sure you can have some. I'll go and sort it out for you. Will you phone Miss Lines, or do you want me to do it?"
"No, I'll phone her. Go and check and see if you've got any Meths will you, and I'll hang on." Francesca went into the stock room and found the liquid, and went back to let her sister know that she could have some. "I'll send one of the juniors along to collect it" she said, "and I'll phone Miss Lines now, and let you know what she says. In the meantime, Fran, what's this I hear about you being taken out in a damn great car?"
"I got taken out for dinner on Saturday night, and the man who took me, owns a really nice Bentley."
"A Bentley!" Samantha exclaimed. "Who is he? Does he have an elder brother?" She laughed and Francesca joined in. "He's the son of one of the patients who was on my ward, and he's only got a sister, so no brothers at all."
"I want to know all about it" her sister said, but Francesca shook her head, even though her sister couldn't see her. "Sorry Sam," she said, "There's not

too much to tell. He's asked me out to dinner, on a few occasions, and I've been and I've thoroughly enjoyed myself."

"Spoilsport" Samantha said, "I'll talk to you soon. Thanks for the Meths, and I'll phone Miss Lines now."

"Thanks Sam. See you soon." and she replaced the receiver. As she did so, she wondered whether the rumours that Ally had heard the night before, had related to the gossip that Sam had heard, and hoped that nothing more would be said, especially when Dominic took her out again. The phone rang again, and this time it was Miss Lines, telling her that Samantha would be lending one of her staff nurses, and one of the student nurses from Exeter Ward would exchange with her, and she would be able to go off duty on time. She was glad to hand over to the girl who came to take over from her, and then to make her way back to the nurses home. She had flung herself down on the bed, wanting to relax, because the day had been long and she was tired. She had pulled off her cap and shoes as she came in, and laid back against the pillows, and was on the verge of dozing off, when Ally knocked on the door and came in. "Oh, my goodness" she said. "You were taken away, we had a round with the new consultant, we still haven't got a replacement for Celia, and Justine went off sick this afternoon, so we've been rushed off our feet."

"So what's the new consultant like?" she asked, and Ally smiled. "Total dreamboat" she said succinctly, "tall, dark and handsome, and his voice, well, its deep and makes you feel as if you're the only woman

in the world, and he's quite young and from what Sister Eames said, he knows exactly what he's talking about."
"So you didn't like him?" Francesca said, with a grin, and Ally laughed. "If I wasn't engaged to Simon, I could make a play for him, but I guess I wouldn't be the only one. The woman who finally gets him, is going to be lucky. He's not wearing a wedding ring, but that doesn't mean a thing – a lot of surgeons don't wear them, so unless somebody asks him, we won't know. It's a shame you weren't on the ward, you could have met him. He hasn't got any patients on the ward yet, but he just inspected a few notes, and had a chat with Mr. Draper and Mr. Rafferty. Sister said he'll be operating on Wednesday so he might appear on the ward on Thursday, and you can meet him then."
"I'm on a half day on Thursday" she said, "so unless he arrives in the morning, I won't see him, but I'm sure I'll meet him soon." she sat up and leaned forward. "Do you want a cuppa?" she asked. "I'm absolutely exhausted as well. I didn't remember what working on a medical ward was like, especially when you're in charge of it. I had to cope with a consultant round this morning, with only a ten-minute warning. It was a nightmare, I'm telling you. You'll be sent next time, I hope. Oh, I meant to tell you. My sister phoned for something they'd run out of, and while she was on the phone, she asked me what the rumours were about me going off in a damn great car. I wondered if that's what you'd heard?"
"Could be" Ally considered that question. "I haven't

heard anything else, so perhaps that's what it was. If he takes you out again, you can tell him he was seen, and tell him that everybody is jealous of you being taken out in a Bentley." She hesitated, then, "Is he taking you out again?" Francesca nodded "Yes, tomorrow night" She grinned at her friend. "I'll tell him that everybody wants a ride in a Bentley and see what he says." She had filled the kettle and plugged it in, and was making the tea as she spoke, and didn't see the smile on the face of her friend. They drank their drinks, before Ally went to her room and Francesca got changed into casual wear. The two girls went down to their supper, but as they entered the dining room, there was a halt in the conversation, and nearly everybody turned to look at the two girls, and Francesca stared at Ally in bewilderment. The talk started again, and the two girls went to the counter to choose their meal, before taking their trays to a spare table. "What was that all about?" she asked, but Ally shook her head. "I've got no idea. Maybe they all fancy a ride in a Bentley." The two girls laughed together, and they finished their meals and went back up to their rooms. "It's getting a bit worrying" Francesca said, but Ally shook her head. "You know what hospitals are like" she said, "people like to gossip about anything and everything. I wouldn't take it seriously if I were you." She grinned at her friend. "Why don't we go out to the cinema?" she said, "we've just got enough time before the main picture starts, and we've both said we wanted to see it." Francesca nodded. "That's a good idea. Grab your coat, and we'll go" and the girls left the nurses home together to walk to the local cinema.

The following day seemed to go very slowly to Francesca, for she was looking forward to the evening which she was going to spend with Dominic. At last, she was off duty, and changing for her date. It was raining, so she wrapped herself in her raincoat, picked up her umbrella, and made her way down to the entrance of the nurses home. The Bentley was parked close to the door, but Dominic was waiting for her, and she was soon in the front seat, being driven away from the hospital. He took her to a restaurant, a distance from the hospital, and she began to wonder why they didn't stay closer, but forgot about that in her delight at seeing him again.
“Have you been busy?” he asked and she nodded.
“Yes”, she said, “I was sent to another ward to work yesterday,” she said. “It was a medical ward, and there was a consultant round which took place about ten minutes after I arrived, and I didn't know the patients or anything about them, so I appeared to be a complete idiot, but luckily the man who did the round was very understanding about the fact that I don't usually work there.”
“So why were you sent?” he asked, and she explained about the Ward Sister's illness, and the fact that the Staff nurses were off duty as well. “I think Miss Lines thought that as I'm nearly qualified – that is, if I pass my exams – I was able to look after the ward. It was good experience for me and I enjoyed it, despite the fact that I was exhausted when I got off duty.” she laughed as she thought of the previous evening. “Ally and I were both off duty in the evening, so we went to the cinema, after we'd

had our supper. But I was going to tell you. Apparently, there have been some odd things being said about me recently. Ally said that she walked into the canteen, and heard my name being mentioned, but when she walked nearer, everybody stopped talking and changed the subject, and then yesterday evening, when she and I walked into the canteen, the room went really quiet, and people were staring at us, then everybody started to talk again. But my sister phoned me yesterday, and asked me what I'd been doing being taken out in a great big car." She grinned at him, "Ally and I reckon that everybody is jealous and they want a ride in your car as well." He smiled at her words, but it was almost as if the smile were forced, but she didn't say anything, and the subject was soon changed. It was as they were driving home after they had eaten their meal, that he asked, "Are you going to be free on Thursday afternoon, or has your duty been changed?" he asked, but she shook her head. "As far as I know, I'll be off on Thursday afternoon." she replied and he smiled at her. "Good. Shall I pick you up from the same place as today at about 1.30?" he asked, "then we can go where we like from there." but she shook her head. "Do you mind if I ask you to meet you outside the post office in the High Street, please, and about 30 minutes later? I've got to send a couple of letters off to our solicitors, and they've got to be registered, and I've forgotten to do them once already, so I've got to do it tomorrow." He grinned at her. "I'm glad to know that it's not only me that forgets things" he said. "I've been wanting to tell you something, but I've never got round to it."

He pulled the car to a halt in a lay by and bent his head to kiss her. When he raised his head again, she was breathless, but his words had made her feel cold inside. He was going to tell her that he was going away, or that he was already married, and she didn't want to hear that. “I've got to tell you something, but I'm not certain how to do it.” he said softly, and pulled her head onto his shoulder. “You're married” she stated, and pulled away from him, but he pulled her back, and rested her head where it had been. “No, I'm certainly not married” he said softly, and kissed her again. “If I was, I wouldn't be doing this. Francesca, you're the only woman I've ever met, who I've felt I could live my life with. I’m not going to say anything yet, because I believe you need some more time, to get to know me better, but believe me, when I feel that you are ready, I won't hesitate.” He kissed her again, and for a while there was silence in the car, but at last he lifted his head from hers, and she felt lost. “No, I've wanted to tell you for a while, but every time I'm with you, I forget things that aren't that important. “What I've got to tell you is” he broke off as his mobile phone rang, and he swore softly as he looked at the number. “Sorry Francesca, I've got to take this. It could be urgent” and he got out of the car, speaking into the phone as he did so. Francesca sat where she was, and looked through the window. He was obviously listening to somebody on the other end of the phone, but now he looked worried, and she wasn't too surprised when he put the phone back in his pocket, and got into the car. “I'm sorry Francesca,” he said, “I've got to get home urgently.” He kissed her once, then put his seat belt on and started the engine, and drove on. They were approaching the hospital, when she said. "Leave me here. It will be quicker for you to go straight home, rather than have to drive around the hospital." and he shot her a glance. "If you don't mind? It would be easier" he said. "I'll see you on Thursday afternoon. Sleep well my darling" and he stopped the car. She got out swiftly, gathered her umbrella and handbag together, said "goodnight," shut the door, and watched him drive away. Slowly, she walked along the street and went into the side entrance of the nurses home, and up to her room. She wondered what he had been about to tell her, but also wanted to know, who had phoned him. She hoped it wasn't anything to do with his father, but she didn't think so, because he would have told her. She would find out tomorrow if the old man was alright. She got ready for bed and was soon lying awake, thinking about Dominic's words. He had intimated that he was going to ask her to marry him, and she knew that if he did, she would accept. He made her feel whole, she loved him, although she had not told him, and he had never told her that he felt the same way about her. She was awake for a long time, thinking about Dominic's words, and wondering exactly what he had been going to tell her.

She was on a late duty the following day, but Sister Eames had phoned the nurses home to ask her if she could go on duty earlier than usual, for there had been a very bad accident on the railway, the night before, and there were a lot of badly injured

patients on the ward, and she knew she was going to be busy. When she went on duty a couple of hours earlier than usual, the ward seemed to be full of people. There were extra beds in the ward, the side wards, which normally had one person in, now had two, and there were a lot of extra nurses on duty. There were quite a few medical staff around as well, and one of the first people she saw was her brother. "Hi Fran" he said. "Lend me a hand please? This guy's pulled his drip out, and I need to get another one in." She willingly agreed, and having caught Sister Eames eye, and let her know that she was on duty, she went behind the curtains with Andy, and gave him some
assistance. She was kept busy after that, running to and fro, keeping an eye on the patients who were seriously ill, and attending to their needs. All the staff worked hard, and she did not get off duty until a lot later than she should have been, by which time she was very tired. By the time she was in bed, she turned over and was asleep within seconds. When the alarm went off, she knew she had to get up immediately, because if she closed her eyes again, she would be asleep again, but knew that she was on a half day and would be able to get some more rest. She was ready for work, pinning her cap on, as Ally knocked on the door, and the two girls went down to the canteen, to make a good meal, before they went on duty. The night report was given to them by Sister Eames, and it took quite a long time. "There are bound to be a lot of consultants coming into the ward today, after yesterday's time in theatre, so when one comes in, make sure that they are

accompanied by somebody senior. If I or Staff Nurse Davies are busy, then I'm going to have to ask either Fran or Ally to take them round." Both girls nodded, and went to make sure that the patients who could eat, could have their breakfast. Fran was helping Justine to roll one of the patients so that they could change the lower sheets, when she heard Sister Eames talking to Mr. Blake, who was the senior consultant. About two minutes later she heard Staff Nurse Davies talking to Mr. Gill, who was another consultant in the department. "Let's hope another consultant doesn't turn up otherwise I'll have to go." she whispered, and Justine smiled at her, "Well there are only another three who are liable to come, so let's hope they don't all turn up at the same time." They were continuing to make the patient comfortable, when they heard the doors swing open again, and Sister's voice calling. "Ally, or Fran, can you come and help please?" Justine smiled at Francesca, and said, "You go, I'll be alright here." Francesca went to the edge of the curtains, and looked out, to see Dominic, wearing a long white coat, and accompanied by Andrew and the house officer, and hurriedly took a step back, only leaning forward to close the curtains properly. "I can't" she whispered, and Justine stared at her white face. "What's the problem?" she asked, but Francesca shook her head and remained silent. "We're a bit tied up in here." Justine called, and Francesca heard Ally say "Good morning. I'm sorry, Sister is a bit busy. I'll look after you if that's okay?" and hurriedly took a deep breath. "I'm sorry Justine" Francesca whispered. "I've just had a shock. I'll be okay in a

bit, but for the moment, I'll stay here."
"I would have thought you would have liked to go round with one of the consultants?" Justine asked. "After all, you'll be qualified seven days time, if you pass, and you'll have to do that."
"I know" she said, in a low voice. "But I won't be doing that with somebody who I know, or at least, I thought I knew." she grinned weakly at the other girl. "I didn't think he had anything to do with the hospital, and now I find he's the new consultant."
Justine looked puzzled, then her face cleared. "Oh," she said, "I thought it was odd you didn't say you were going out with him. We all knew you were, but as you didn't say anything, neither did anybody else. Obviously, you met him, when his step father was a patient." she looked at Francesca. "Didn't he tell you he was coming to work here?" Francesca shook her head, then turned her attention back to the patient, so that when Sister put her head around the curtains to see if they were ready to be seen by Mr. Blake, she was able to nod, and assist with the visit. She stayed with him, until Sister sent her to accompany one of the other registrars who was visiting the ward, and she did so, not looking at Dominic, as he made his way around the ward, looking at some of the patients who had been operated on the day before. Sister was still busy with Mr. Blake, so when the phone in the office rang, as it had been doing all morning, Francesca went to answer it. She was noting the results of one of the blood tests that had been done that morning, when Dominic appeared in the doorway of the office, along with Andy and Ally. She finished noting the results,

read them back, to make sure they were correct, and had replaced the receiver, when Ally led Dominic and Andy into to the office. “Hi Fran” Andrew said, then turned to the tall man beside him, “Dominic, this is my sister, Fran. Fran, this is our new consultant Mr. Cavanagh”. Francesca stared at him, she had regained her colour now, but didn't know what to say. “We've already met” she said eventually, “Will you excuse me please, I've got to give these blood results to Sister.” and she walked away from the group. She was able to keep away from him after that, instead making sure that she was able to attend to the patients, several of whom needed extra care, but as she worked, she realised exactly why she had been talked about. The silence when she entered the canteen made sense now, obviously somebody had seen Dominic pick her up outside the nurses home, and then she remembered Janet's words, about not having wasted any time, and her face flushed. He was meant to be taking her out that afternoon, but she doubted he would be able to leave the hospital, for he had several patients on the ward, and none of them were very well. She resigned herself to having to stay on duty, but when the rounds were finished, and Sister came to find her, she was reminded that she was on a half day. “Go off duty Fran. We'll be able to cope now. We've coped before and we will again. Thank you for your help yesterday and today.”
“Are you sure you don't want me to stay?” she asked, but the older woman shook her head. “No my dear, that's alright. Go and enjoy your afternoon off.” and she smiled at her, so that Francesca knew

she would have to go. She didn't want to go back to the nurses home – she wanted to go somewhere quiet and think about the events of the morning. She remembered that she had to go to the Post Office, and when the time came, she went off duty, got changed, and went out again. She didn't have to wait too long for service, and she slowly walked along the High Street, going back to the Nurses home, when the Bentley slid to a silent halt beside her. "Get in" Dominic said, as he opened the door for her, and without a word, she did so. "I'm sorry" he said softly, as she did her seat belt up. "I was going to tell you last night." She was silent for a while, not knowing what to say, until she recognised the streets they were driving through, until they drew up outside the house she had lived in for so long, and left so recently. "Oh, that's really great" she said bitterly. "Not only do you work in the same hospital as I do, which you didn't tell me, you let me tell you all about the new consultant and how we wanted to know if he'd be kind to students, and then I find out it's you, you let me be the butt of everybody's gossip, and now I find that you are the new owner of my old house. I'm sorry Dominic, I can't do this anymore." and she put her hand on the handle to get out, but he stopped her, and pulled her back into his arms. "I wanted to tell you" he said, "and I was about to, when the phone rang, if you remember. I was going to tell you everything. I'd obviously never met you, because you didn't show me round the house when it was for sale, you left that to the estate agents, so we didn't get a chance to meet then, but then we met when Dad was in hospital, and I wanted to take you out, so I invited you, and you came with me. You never asked me what I did, although I'd told you I'd been teaching and doing research when I lived in New Zealand, and I realised you had no idea that I was about to start at the hospital. You obviously know now why everybody stopped talking when you went into the canteen – they wanted to see you, because it's not often that a new consultant starts taking a student nurse out, before he even starts work." He smiled slightly, "You were very short when Andrew introduced us this morning." he said softly, and the hard lump that was inside her throat seemed to melt slightly, and she felt tears come to her eyes. Dominic saw them as well, and drew her towards him, and gently kissed them away. "Don't cry darling" he kissed her then, and she felt her anger subside. "Come inside and see what I've done" he said, and got out and came round to open her door for her. He led her inside, and she looked around. The hallway was the same – but had been re-papered in a light-coloured paper, the woodwork was white, and the carpet was a dark green – the same as it had been, but it was newer, and looked as it had done, when she looked back into the past, and saw how it had been when she was a little girl. He took her hand and led her into the sitting room, which had been a dark forbidding place, with lots of furniture, and she had been surprised when the van had taken away all the old tables and chairs, to see how big the room actually was. Now, she got another surprise. The sitting room was lighter in colour than it had been – one wall, the wall around the fireplace, had been

painted in a cream colour, and the others were painted in a pale blue. There were long blue curtains at the windows, and the floor which had been carpeted, was now showing off the oak boards which had been underneath it, but had now been polished, with several rugs in front of the fire, and around the room. There were two settees at right angles to the fireplace, and a Welsh dresser stood against one wall, with a dinner service displayed on the shelves. There were a couple of small tables around, and Francesca looked around her. "There's a bit more furniture due to be delivered quite soon" he said "but this room is peaceful and very restful. I like it very much."
"It's lovely" she said. "Mum had too much furniture in here – she wouldn't get rid of anything that had belonged to my father and some of it was really ancient, and very uncomfortable. There was an old settee that had belonged to my fathers' mother, which had two springs coming through the cover, but she wouldn't let anybody repair it, and I couldn't wait to get rid of it." He grinned, and pulled her towards him, holding her close, as he kissed her. "I had met your sister when we were negotiating when I was buying the house, but I didn't meet your brother, until we were in the solicitor's office together, when we had to sign some papers, and I only met him properly for the first time, when we were introduced when I was shown round the hospital. And then you told me all about him, and I realised that you were related to him. I didn't know, honestly, I just thought the name was the same, and it was a coincidence." He kissed her again, and held

her close. “Am I forgiven?” he asked her and she nodded. “It was such a shock, when I looked out of the curtains round the patients bed, and saw you on the ward.” she said. “I heard Sister calling Ally or myself, I went to look through the curtains, and saw you, and I couldn't have taken you on a round feeling as I did. Sorry Dominic.”

“As I said, I was going to tell you on Tuesday night, when Andrew phoned. I hadn't told you anything, and I didn't want you to find out from listening to my answers on a phone call.” He smiled at her. “So, if I'm definitely forgiven, will you spend the afternoon and evening with me? Andrew is on duty, and I’m on call, but I shouldn’t be called in. I'll show you around the house, show you what I've done so far, and we can talk, if that would be okay?”

She nodded, her eyes bright as he kissed her again, and knew she felt extremely happy. “I'd like that” she said, before he kissed her again, and he grinned. “So will I my darling girl. So will I.”

Chapter Five

By the time Dominic took her back to the Nurses Home, that evening, Francesca felt very much better. She had spent the afternoon and evening with him, they had talked about anything and everything, and she knew she loved him more than ever. His kiss, before he had taken her back, had made her realise she wanted him to continue holding her, kissing her, and she gasped as she realised, she wanted to stay with him, not just for that time, but for always. He had taken her on a tour of the house, to show her what he had altered, and introduced her to his housekeeper – Mrs Bradley, who she had met several times in the past when she had accompanied her mother to visit friends. Mrs. Bradley had been their housekeeper, but now she had left their employ and she was working for Dominic, and she had told Francesca she was very happy to be looking after him. "It's a meeting of old friends, isn't it?" Dominic had said, and Francesca had smiled at him. "I'm glad that you were the buyer" she said, when they were alone again. "The house was much too big for me alone, which I knew, but wouldn't admit it, but it had so many memories, I didn't really want to leave it. I was born in it, after all." He had looked at her. "Were you?" he asked, "I didn't know. What happened?"

"Mum went into early labour when I was due, but she couldn't get hold of my father, because he was busy at the hospital, and she didn't want to call an ambulance, so when my father finally got the message that he was needed at home, it was too late to get her to the hospital, and I was born in the room that is now your bedroom." He had kissed her then, and smiled. "So this house really is part of you" he said, before taking her hand and leading her into the sitting room. They had taken seats on one of the settees, and now he pulled her into his arms, and kissed her again and again. They had ended up lying together, his arms holding her close to him, and she felt safe. "When do you get your results?" he asked her, after a minute, and she had opened her eyes wide. "On Thursday, if the postman delivers them" she said, "but there's been a strike remember, so goodness knows when they'll turn up. I suppose Miss Lines might get told, before we do, but I'm not certain. Why do you want to know?"

"Because I want to take you out to celebrate, and I can't do that if I'm on call."

"I might not pass anyway" she said, but he shook his head. "I don't think you will fail" he said. "Sister Eames told me that she fully expects you to pass with flying colours. Apparently, you've done well in all your exams so far, and she expects you to be in line for one of the medals."

She looked at him, her eyes questioning "Sister Eames said that?" she asked and he nodded. "Everybody expects you to pass, so I reckon you will. You must have been having a very bad day on the day of the exam if you fail. So, where am I going to take you to celebrate? Where do you want to go?"

"I haven't the faintest idea" she said. "Before you started taking me out and about, I didn't go anywhere, and as Sam and Andy will be working on that day, I won't be able to go out with them. We

were talking about having a party if we all pass, but I've heard nothing more about that idea."
"Do you fancy going back to the Hayrack again, if I can get a table?" he asked her and she nodded. "I'd love it. I really enjoyed my last visit. Thank you," and she kissed him gently. He had returned the embrace, and she laid back against the cushions and looked up at him. He bent and kissed her again, his hands holding her close, gently touching her breasts, and she allowed him to do so, although the breath caught in her throat as he touched her. "You've never done anything like this before have you?" he said quietly, and she shook her head. "No" she whispered, and he moved his hands away. "Plenty of time in the future" he said quietly, before he sat up and pulled her into a sitting position. "We'll have something to eat, then have a drink, and I'll take you back to the nurses home." And that is what they had done. When she got ready for bed that evening, back in the Nurses Home, she remembered all he had said and done, and knew that she was happy when she was with him, and she was looking forward to the future, a future she was sure would hold Dominic.

She had gone on duty, and Sister Eames had asked her to accompany Mr. Gill on his round, Ally was on a day off. She knew she was able to do it, but was grateful that Sister was accompanying her, for the old surgeon was in a very bad mood, and spent the entire time moaning about things that had happened or not been done, on the ward. By the time it finished, she was glad that she wasn't going

to be on the ward if she passed, because he had made her feel as if she knew nothing and she felt really stupid after listening to his comments. She was nervous about the following days, for her results were due, and she was hoping that they were going to be delivered early, for the post lately was very unpredictable. When she finally got off duty that evening, she was tired, but after a quick bath, she was relaxed enough to think about going downstairs to the canteen. She looked in her bag to find her purse, and realised that neither her purse or her phone was there. Puzzled now, she looked again, and realised that she hadn't looked into her bag since her break, for she had paid for her lunch and put her purse back into her bag. She had put the bag into the office, in the cupboard they all used to store personal equipment, and locked it back up again, before collecting it at the end of the day, and realised that somebody had stolen her belongings. She hadn't seen anybody strange in the ward that afternoon, for there hadn't been visiting that afternoon, and wondered who could have taken them. She hurried to the internal phone, and phoned the ward. Sister Eames was still on duty, and answered at the second ring. "Sister, it's Fran" she began and was surprised to hear the other woman say wearily, "oh not you as well."
"I take it I'm not the only person to have found that my purse and phone has been taken from my bag?" she asked, and heard the woman say "Yes. Everybody has lost their purses, and I think three phones were taken."
"Who on earth could it have been?" Francesca asked

"I didn't see anybody strange in the ward this afternoon, did you?"
"No. I was in the office for most of the afternoon, and only out of it for just twenty or thirty minutes when I was at a meeting with Miss Lines. We were in her office for fifteen minutes before I returned to the ward. Fran, I have to ask, have you lost any credit or debit cards, because if you have, then you need to cancel them immediately?"
"No, because I live in, I only bring some cash to work with me. I didn't lose much, but the phone has gone, and there weren't that many contact numbers on that either." she hesitated, "did you lose anything?" and was surprised to hear the other woman sniff back a tear. "Yes," she said, "my purse was taken, all my cards, but most distressing, my photos of my daughter were in there, and I haven't got many of them anyway." Francesca knew that Sister Eames had lost a daughter when she was only two, and knew the loss this would cause. "I'm sorry Sister" she said softly. "Do you need any cash urgently, because if so, then I can get it from the cash machine, and bring it to you."
"That's very kind of you to offer Fran, but not to worry. My husband is sorting everything out with the bank, I've reported it to the hospital authorities and the police have been contacted already and are here trying to find out who took it. Sleep well Fran, and good luck for the day after tomorrow. We'll see you when you come in."
"Thanks Sister. See you." she replaced the receiver, and went back to her room, to seek out some money from the stash she kept, for she had got into the

habit of taking very little on duty with her, just in case of a loss, such as this one, and went down to the canteen. The talk there was all about the theft, and she kept well out of it, not wanting to get involved. The next day, she had to go and purchase a new mobile phone, and set about giving everybody the new number. She had tried to phone Dominic, but his voicemail box was full, and she didn't have his home phone number, his secretary wasn't available, so hadn't been able to contact him, so deciding that she would have to ask Andy to do it for her, she phoned his home, and had to leave a message, as both he and Theresa were out. She had phoned Sam, but she wasn't in either, so left her number on her machine as well, and asked her to phone her. That evening, she walked to Dominic's house, and put a letter telling him what had happened, with her new phone number through the letter box, and went back to the nurses home. The following day, her results were due out, and she was very tense, as she awaited the arrival of the postman. Her friends in the same set were in a similar situation, and as they had been given time off to wait for the postman, they were sitting together, as they waited for their results. At last, the Home Sister came to tell them, that the postman had been, and they went to collect their letters. Everybody, apart from Francesca, received a brown envelope, but there was nothing for her, and she congratulated her friends, but sat silently, watching her friends celebrate. At last, Ally, a large smile on her face, looked at her. “Well,” she said, “Did you pass?”
“I don't know,” she said, “I haven't had an

envelope." Her friends looked at her. "Why on earth not?" they asked, but she had no answer. "I asked Home Sister, and she tells me that there isn't any more post. I'm going to phone Miss Lines, and see if she's been given any information." Her friends waited with her, as she made the call, but the nursing officer didn't have any other information. "I haven't received the list I should have done, so I don't know who passed or failed," she admitted to Francesca. "Are you the only one who's not received an envelope?"

"The only one." admitted Francesca. "I don't know what to do now. I might have to wait until tomorrow, to see if the post comes."

"If I hear anything else, I'll let you know." Miss Lines promised, and with that, Francesca had to be satisfied. "Looks like you are going to be able to celebrate after all" she said with a forced smile to Ally. "Enjoy yourselves tonight won't you," she said, "I'll go back to the ward, and get some work done. I'll see you." and she walked slowly away, wondering what could have happened to her results. It was while she was walking past the offices when Miss Lines approached her. "Fran, I'm sorry I can't find out your results. They are having problems with the phone lines; they're constantly engaged with other people trying to get through." Francesca smiled sadly at her, the nursing officer told her she would do her best to find out the results, and Francesca went on her way back to the ward. When she walked onto the ward, her sad face made Sister Eames look twice at her. "What happened?" she asked. "You couldn't have failed, surely?"

“I don't know” she admitted. “My results haven't arrived. Everybody else's did, and they are all celebrating tonight, but my envelope didn't arrive, and Miss Lines has told me that her copy of the results hasn't arrived either, and she can't get through on the phone.”
“Oh Francesca, as if we haven't had enough problems lately. What do you want to do? Do you want to work, or take the rest of the day off?”
“I'd rather work” she said, “hopefully my envelope will arrive tomorrow, and I'll find out. In the meantime, what do you want me to do?” Sister gave her a list of things to be getting on with, and glad to be doing something that would keep her mind off the events of the morning, she got on with the work. She was waiting for Dominic to phone her that evening, and hopefully they would be going out, for she had put a note with her new phone number through his door, and knew he would have found it by now. She waited for a phone call, but there was nothing. Her friends all of whom had passed, came to see her, commiserating with her about the fact that the all-important envelope hadn't turned up, before they went out for a meal, to celebrate together, and Francesca was left alone, to sit in the dark, listening to the radio, and wonder why Dominic hadn't phoned her.

The following morning, she went into work, but was given permission to go over to the home, and see if the post had arrived, which she did, but there was still no news for her. That evening, Ally was packing to go home, for three weeks leave, which

most of her friends would have, before they started work again, and she didn't have anybody to talk to, as all of her friends were in similar circumstances.
"You will let me know what happens, won't you?" Ally asked, and Francesca reassured her that she would do so. "When I get my results, I'll let you know" she said, and with that, the other girl had to be satisfied. "I'm sure they'll come through soon" she reassured her, "and in the meantime, we've got our party to look forward to."
"No we haven't" Ally told her. "Didn't anybody tell you? Geraldine was meant to have arranged everything, but she forgot to book the party room, and it's not available."
"Oh great" Francesca said bitterly. "That explains why you're all going home, but it means I won't see any of you again, until you get back and start your new jobs. Of course I might have failed, in which case, I'll still be here, and working for the next lot of exams."
"Don't be daft" Ally said. "Of course you've passed, and if you haven't you must have had a very bad day on the day of the exam, and I don't think you did. It's just a glitch in the system, I'm sure of it." her friend told her, before getting ready to go back to her room. "I'm going to be leaving very early in the morning" she said, "so I'll say goodbye now, and I'm sure we'll be able to meet up again, when I get back." Francesca and Ally exchanged goodbyes and Ally went back to her room. Francesca stared after her, wondering what had changed between them, for there was a reserve that hadn't been there before, and she wondered whether it was the fact

that her friends were now staff nurses, and she was still a student nurse and she regretted the change in their relationship.

By the time Saturday morning came around, Francesca was on edge. She wasn't due to work again, unless she had failed the exams, so didn't have to go onto the ward. Dominic hadn't contacted her, and although she had phoned him on more than one occasion, but he hadn't responded, and she hadn't been able to leave a message, because the voicemail inbox was still full. She had tried to phone his secretary, to ask her to pass on the message, but the woman only worked Monday to Wednesday, and there was no answer, and the answer phone didn't activate. She was sitting on the edge of her bed, wondering when the post would arrive, when the Home Sister came and knocked on her door. She was waving a brown envelope, and eagerly Francesca opened it, and found that it was indeed her results, and she had passed with flying colours. There was another envelope for her as well, this time from the hospital, telling her she was the Gold Medallist for the year, and her job in theatres would start in three weeks time. She had phoned Samantha, but she still wasn't in, and Andrew wasn't picking up either, and she sat and wept, because she wanted to tell somebody the good news, and there wasn't anybody to tell. She wanted to let Dominic know, but the phone remained unanswered, and she wondered what had changed in their relationship. She knew she wasn't able to go anywhere else, and wondered what she was going to do with three

weeks leave. She wanted to go and see her sister, but Samantha didn't seem to be available, and when she phoned the ward, she was told her sister was on a fortnight's holiday, so she resigned herself to spending the time in her room, or just visiting places near the hospital. She went downstairs to get some lunch in the canteen, but didn't see anybody she knew, so went to the cemetery where her parents were buried, and standing by their grave, and placing some flowers on it, she told them the news, but knew she'd have to go back, and walked slowly through the streets to the hospital, and when she got back to her room, she found the Home Sister waiting to talk to her. "Fran, I'm really sorry" she began, and Francesca knew something else bad was going to happen. "I've been asked to tell you that you can't stay in your room for your leave. The new intake is going to be moving in very soon, and they want to keep them all together, and they're going to be put in these rooms. You'll be moving into one of the Staff Nurses Rooms on the third floor, but I'm afraid that there won't be one ready until your leave ends. I'm really very sorry, Fran. You're going to have to find somewhere else to stay, because we don't have any spare rooms in the home. You can put your belongings in the store room. If you could move out this weekend, we'd be very grateful."
"Oh great" Fran said, bitterly. "Thanks a lot. Where am I meant to go?" she asked, "If you remember, I had to move in here, because our house was being sold. I haven't got anywhere else I can go."
"Couldn't you go and stay with your sister or your brother?" the Home Sister asked, and Francesca

stared at her, resentful at the news. “I suppose so” she said, knowing she wouldn't able to do any such thing, for she was still unable to contact Samantha or her brother, and Home Sister smiled, knowing that she had made a sensible suggestion, but unaware that Francesca wasn't able to contact anybody. Francesca looked after the other woman as she left the room, having delivered the bad news, and knew she was completely fed up with life in general. Everything seemed to be going wrong lately. She was in a very bad mood as she got out her cases, wondering what else could go wrong, and started to pack everything up. She put some clothes into a separate bag, then, took everything else down to the store room, made sure that she had her credit card in her wallet, and handing in the keys to the home warden, she left the room, and headed towards the station, determined to go somewhere, anywhere, away from the hospital.

When she got to the station, she looked at the destination board and found that a train was due. It said that it was headed to York, and as she had been there with her mother, and been happy there, she knew she could be again, so she purchased her ticket and got onto the train. A couple of hours later, the train ran into York station, and she pulled her case after her, and left the station. She knew there was a big hotel nearby, and not caring too much about the cost, she walked into the foyer to book a room. By the time she had unpacked her case, eaten a meal from room service and had a long hot bath, she was ready for bed, and she curled up under the covers, and too tired to think, she was soon asleep.

It was nearly a week since her results had been announced, and still nobody had contacted her. She hadn't expected to hear from Andy, for her brother was notorious for not contacting anybody, but she thought Sam might had made an effort and done so, so she had phoned several times, leaving her number on the machine again, in case Sam hadn't made a note of it, but had still not heard anything from her sister, but she was very hurt that Dominic, who had been so eager to hear whether she had passed or not, when she had been on the ward, hadn't contacted her at all. She had tried to phone his secretary, but the woman was never present, and the answer machine didn't seem to be working. There seemed to be a large lump in her chest that hurt, when she thought about him, and knew she was missing him very badly, but supposed she would have to get used to that, if he truly didn't want to retain their contact. She had made herself go out and about, but she was lonely, without anybody to talk to, and realised it had been a mistake to come back to the city. She wasn't eating or sleeping properly, had lost weight, and she was tired of crying herself to sleep every night, so nearly a week after she arrived, she made another effort, and phoned all three. She couldn't contact Dominic, for he still wasn't available, and the answer machine in his office still wasn't working, Andrew wasn't available on his bleep, Theresa wasn't in, and she left yet another message on the machine, but doubted whether Andrew would hear it, for she didn't think

Theresa would draw his attention to it. Lastly, she phoned Samantha, and was very pleased when her sister actually answered her phone. “Sam, its Fran” she said, and nearly had her hearing blown away by her sister’s answer. “Fran! Where the hell are you? What's happened, why didn't you phone me, and why aren't you still in the Nurses Home? Home Sister said you'd left, but you hadn't said where you were going. She thought you were coming to stay with me or Andy, and he hasn't heard from you.”

“I had my phone stolen from the ward, so I had to go and buy a new one. and then I got told I couldn't stay in the nurses home for my leave. I thought you might have phoned me, but you didn't.”

“I didn't have your new number” Sam said. “I've been phoning you every day for a week, but obviously it wasn't being answered, if it was stolen. But why didn't you let me know the new one?”

“I did, at least three times” she insisted. “I left the new number on your answer machine every time. Why don't you ever check it?”

“There's been nothing left on my machine for a week or two. I've been away staying with a friend, and there weren't any messages at all when I got back. But what happened with the exam? Did you pass?”

“Yes,” she said coldly, “I did. I also got the gold medal, but as nobody seemed to want to talk to me, I haven't been able to tell anybody.”

“But why aren't you in the nurses home? Where are you?”

“I'm in my bedroom in a hotel in York” she announced.

"York?" exclaimed Sam. "Why York? You don't know anybody in York. What are you doing up there anyway?"
"I was informed that I couldn't stay in the nurses home, after I'd passed my exams, because my new room as a staff nurse wouldn't be ready for three weeks, and they required my old one, for the new intake, and there weren't any spare rooms available. They asked me to leave the Home as soon as possible. I've stored my stuff, and as I don't have anywhere else to go, because you and Andy insisted that we sold the house, and as I couldn't contact you to ask if I could stay with you, I had to go away, so I got on a train and here I am in York." She didn't care that she sounded sarcastic when mentioning her siblings decision, for she was aware that Sam knew how she felt about it.
"Oh Fran, I'm so sorry. I didn't know they'd asked you to leave the home. But congratulations on passing and getting the medal. Did you have a good celebration with your friends?"
"No." she said shortly, "I haven't celebrated at all, unless you count the glass of very indifferent, very expensive wine, I treated myself to, when I arrived here at the hotel. We were going to go for a meal, on the night we got the results, but my results didn't come through until two days later, so all my friends who'd got their results, went out that evening, and I just sat in the home, wondering why mine hadn't arrived, and not being able to tell anybody about it either, because I couldn't contact anybody."
"I'm sorry Fran, as I said, I was away with some friends." Sam said, but Fran wasn't really listening

and continued. "Anyway, all my friends went home for their leave, and I stayed at the home, because I didn't know whether I could celebrate or not. We were going to have a party, but the girl who was organising it, forgot to book the room in the nurses home, and it wasn't available, so we didn't have a party either, which is why everybody went home."
"But what about your friend, the one with the Bentley? Didn't he take you out?"
"No. He hasn't contacted me. I suppose he had to work, because he's the new Orthopaedic consultant. I had no idea, and although he was going to tell me, he couldn't, as he was called in to deal with the victims of the train crash, I got the surprise of my life when I saw him walk onto the ward to do a round of his patients. He is also the man who bought our house, and he's Andy's new boss. I've was trying to get in touch with him, because he said he was interested, but he's never able to answer his phone, and the voicemail box is full, so I went to the house, and left him a note with the new number in it, but he's never contacted me, so I don't think he wants to continue our friendship. It was nice while it lasted though."
"You were going out with Dominic Cavanagh?" Samantha sounded as if she were smiling. "Of course, we met him when he was buying the house, and he came to the solicitors to sign the paperwork. You weren't there at that time. But Fran, you said he was taking you out right until the exam results came out. Maybe he hasn't got your phone number, maybe the note got lost, or something like that."
"I thought of that, so when I left the message with

my new phone number on Andy's answer machine, I asked Andy to give him the number as well, so there have been plenty of opportunities for him to use it, but he hasn't phoned, so I think that's it now."
"So you didn't celebrate at all?" Sam asked her and Francesca replied, bitterly, "No, but that's been the story of my life lately, hasn't it? Didn't even see any of my friends, when the results eventually came through, because they'd all left by then. Even Miss Lines didn't know whether I'd passed or failed, because the post was up the creek, because of the strike. And to put the tin lid on everything, I phoned Ally to let her know, but she's gone on holiday with her fiancée, so I haven't even been able to tell her."
"Oh Fran, I'm so sorry." Samantha said. "Come home, and you can stay here. We can go out for a meal to celebrate."
"No thanks Sam, thanks for the offer, but I'm going to move on tomorrow, go and see some other places that I visited with mum. I've been told I can move into my new room, in two weeks time, just before I start work, so I'll be back then. Don't worry Sam, I'll be okay. I've got to be, haven't I? I'll phone you again next week. Bye", and she pressed the button to disconnect. She would have been very surprised to see how her sister sprang into action. She made a note of the phone number, then phoned her brother in the hospital. For a change, he was available, and he answered his phone, and listened to his sister telling him off, for not having congratulated his youngest sister on passing her exam and getting the gold medal and told him what had happened. "She never got a phone call from you, despite the fact that

she left you her new phone number, and told you that her phone had been stolen, and don't tell me that your answer machine isn't working, because I talked to Theresa yesterday, after she phoned me back, when I left a message on the machine. I'll bet she didn't tell you that Fran had phoned, did she?" Samantha was very annoyed now, and Andy acknowledged that his wife was the probable culprit.

"And," she went on, "can you ask Dominic Cavanagh why he didn't have the courtesy to tell Fran that he didn't want to see her again?"

"Why does Dominic want to see her again? They didn't seem to be very friendly when I introduced them when I took him onto the ward after the train crash. She said she'd met him already, but they didn't seem to be getting on very well."

"He's been taking her out for the last few weeks." Samantha said angrily. "He told her he wanted to know when she got her results, because he was going to take her out to celebrate, but he hasn't done that, and he's really hurt her" and she told him of Fran's efforts to contact him. "You've got to talk to him, and ask him why he doesn't want to see her again."

"I can't ask him that Sam. He's my boss, and you don't ask your boss why he doesn't want to see a woman again, even if that woman is your sister. He's been really bad tempered lately, and I don't want to upset him even more."

"Maybe not, but poor Fran deserves some kindness in her life at the moment. Her exam results were delayed, so she didn't get them until a couple of days after everybody else, which meant she wasn't able to go out to celebrate with her friends that evening. Apparently, she didn't even manage to get to a party with her friends, because they weren't able to have one. How would you have felt if you hadn't been able to celebrate after you passed your exams? I know exactly how I would have felt! And if I remember correctly, your celebration party went on for about three days! By the time her results did arrive, all of her friends had left and gone to their homes, so she wasn't able to tell anybody, even her best friend Ally wasn't in when she phoned and has gone on holiday, so she can't talk to her, I was away, she couldn't contact you, and now she's been stood up by Dominic. I only found out just now, that she'd been seeing him. I didn't know either, that she was going to be chucked out of the nurses home, until her new room is ready, so she had nowhere to go, because as she said, you and I insisted we sold the house, and I didn't get her phone call to tell me her new number. I don't think we've treated Fran very well lately, Andy. As the youngest child, she was always so close to mum, working with her as well, so when she died, it must have hurt Fran much more than it hurt you or I. And then, you listened to Theresa telling you that you were entitled to your share of the house, and we forced her to agree to putting the house on the market. You've got somewhere to live with Theresa, I've bought my flat, but she's got nowhere, and if I'd known she had to leave the nurses home, I'd have made her come and stay with me, but I didn't, and so she's disappeared off to stay in a hotel, with nobody to talk to. At the very least, I think she's owed an apology from Dominic."

Andy agreed with her – he hadn't realised just what had happened, and he'd felt slightly worried that Fran had been left without anywhere to go, when Theresa had pressured him into discussing the matter with Samantha, and selling the house, and he was suspicious that Theresa hadn't passed on the information that Fran had phoned. He determined to go home that evening and confront his wife.
"What's her new phone number?" he asked now, and Samantha read it out to him. "I'll phone her," he said, and Sam wondered whether he would. "Just talk to Dominic Cavanagh and give him the number," she ordered. "Or I'll phone him and tell him what I think of him, and I might be extremely rude to him." and she disconnected. Andy looked at the phone, listening to the dialling tone, and knowing his sister of old. She would probably be extremely rude to his new boss, and he didn't want to be around if she was. He walked back into the surgeons' room, and found Dominic sitting at the desk, going through some notes. His boss had been really bad tempered recently, and the young registrar was very reluctant to talk to him about matters which could be the cause of it. "Dominic" he said hesitantly, "Don't shout at me. This is not my idea. I've just had a phone call from my sister Sam. She's really cross with you, and she's told me to tell you that you've got to apologise to Fran. She said it was extremely discourteous of you not to tell her that you didn't want to see her again, just drop her without saying a word, and I hate to say it, but I think I agree with her." Dominic stared at his registrar. "Don't talk such rot" he said angrily, "I do want to see her

again.” he disagreed with his registrar's statement. “I have absolutely no idea where she is. She's disappeared into thin air. She's not in the nurses home any more, and nobody has any idea where she's gone. I don't even know if she passed her exams. As you know, I had to take over from Mr. Gill at a moment’s notice, so I wasn't able to take her out to celebrate, if she'd passed, but she's never contacted me, and her phone's not being answered, and I've rung her more times than I care to mention.”
“She did pass her exams, and she also got the Gold medal apparently, but she was told she had to leave the nurses home and go somewhere else, because her room was needed for the new set. But her phone was stolen, and she's had to get a new one, and she left the new number on our answering machine, and asked me to pass it on to you, but I didn't get that message. Sam's machine isn't working properly, apparently, and she didn't know that Fran wasn't in contact with anybody.”
“Well, why didn't she let me know her new number?” Dominic asked the young registrar.
“She tried, apparently, but your voicemail box is full, and she couldn't leave a message. But she said she went to your house and put a note through the door, giving you the new number. I don't know what happened to it.”
“Where is she?” Dominic asked, but Andrew didn't know. “Sam didn't tell me,” he answered. “She just said she'd gone to stay in a hotel for a while, and told me off for not contacting her. Apparently, she didn't get her results until two days after the rest of the girls in her set, so she hasn't managed to celebrate at

all."
"Oh, poor Francesca." Dominic shook his head. It seemed that events had conspired against Francesca, and he was eager to talk to her. "Give me her phone number please Andrew. I'll phone her now, and apologise to her." The information was given, and Andy decided to go and leave his boss alone. Dominic looked around him, and decided this probably wasn't the best place to phone Francesca. He could be interrupted at any time, so he got up, walked to his office, shutting the door behind him, and sitting down at his desk, he dialled Francesca's number. It was answered at the second ring, and Francesca sounded a bit wary as she answered. "Hello" she said. "Francesca?" said Dominic, "Oh Francesca my darling, where are you? I've been trying to contact you for over a week now, and of course your phone was never answered. Samantha ordered Andrew to let me have your new number, and he's just done that. Francesca my darling, I've missed you so much. What happened? By the time we'd sorted out Mr. Gill's patients and lists, you'd disappeared and I couldn't contact you."
Francesca listened to Dominic's voice, and the lump in her chest seemed to dissolve a little. She was crying, as she told him the full story, how her purse and phone had been stolen, how she'd left the number on both Samantha's and Andrew's answering machines, and how she'd been trying to let him know, by phone and by leaving a note at the house, but nobody had contacted her. When she got to the end of the story, she was sobbing bitterly, and he wanted to be able to take her in his arms and

comfort her. "Don't cry my darling, but come home, come and stay with me, Mrs. Bradley will love to look after you in the day time, if I have to work, and I can look after you in the evenings. And I can take you out to celebrate passing your exams as well. You poor thing, not being able to celebrate at all! I can't believe the nurses home made you leave until your new room was available. I would never have let you go away, if you'd been able to tell me. Oh, Francesca my darling girl, I've missed you so much, and I've got so much to tell you and ask you. Please say you'll come home."
Francesca nodded. She was lonely, didn't like being on her own in a city so far from everything and everybody she knew, and now she understood that he hadn't wanted to break up with her, she felt better. "Can I really stay with you?" she asked and he smiled. "Of course you can darling, you can even have your old bedroom if you want. Will you come home tomorrow, because I think it might be a bit late tonight."
"I'll leave the hotel in the morning, and get a train. I should be back in the afternoon, if that would be okay. I'll get a taxi to the house, and meet you there if Mrs. Bradley is at home, and can let me in, so I'll be waiting for you when you get home."
"No my darling, phone me, and let me know what time your train gets in, and I'll meet you on the station. I want to see you as soon as possible, so I'll be waiting for you." They talked for quite a while, before they said their farewells, and Dominic cleared the old messages from his in box, and knew he had been guilty of not doing so before. By the time he

was able to leave and go home that evening, he was wondering about the disappearance of Francesca's note, and as soon as he got in, went straight to the study, to look on the desk, in case Mrs. Bradley had put it on there. He had been hunting for a while, when he found it. His housekeeper had placed it on the desk, but it had had been caught up in some magazines, and he realised the number had been on his desk all the time. He hoped he would be able to make everything up to Francesca, and knew he was going to ask her to marry him as soon as he could.

Chapter Six

The train from York was late, and Francesca was extremely pleased when it finally drew into the station. She was one of a handful of passengers who got out, and she looked to see which way to go to the exit, but before she could take another step, she was caught, held close and then kissed by Dominic. The kiss lasted a long time, and she didn't want to move out of his arms. "Oh my darling Francesca" he muttered, when he lifted his head, before kissing her again. "I've missed you so much. Come, let me take you home, and you can tell me what's been happening" and he took her case, led her through the station exit and out to where the Bentley was waiting. He handed her in, put the case in the boot, then came to sit beside her, but he didn't start the engine immediately, instead, bending his head to kiss her again. "Let's go home" he said quietly, and turned the key to start the engine. They didn't speak as he drove home, for Francesca couldn't think of anything to say that didn't demand an explanation, and she didn't want to ask for one, as he was driving. As they drew up outside his house, she smiled at him, and got out, and he led her to the front door. Dominic led her into the sitting room, shut the door behind them, and took her in his arms again. When he finally lifted his head, she was dizzy from the amount of emotion she had experienced.
"Francesca, I'm so sorry I wasn't able to see you on Thursday evening." he said. "I had to go and take over from Mr. Gill. He had a major heart attack that afternoon. He hadn't been feeling very well for a

couple of days, but didn't say anything to anybody, and collapsed as he was walking into theatre. His patients were ready for surgery, and couldn't be cancelled at such short notice, so the rest of us surgeons had to stand in for him. I couldn't get in touch with you, and when I finally got out of theatre, it was too late to try again. And the following day, was the same." Francesca nodded. "That explains the way he was treating me, when I took him round the day before." she said. "He was evil towards me and towards the patients, we couldn't do anything right, and now I know why." Dominic kissed her and continued. "I couldn't contact you; I did try several times before I went into theatre, and again when I'd finished the operation, but I know now, your phone had been stolen, and nobody had your new number." Francesca drew back from his embrace. "But they did" she argued. "I left a message on Andy's answering machine, asking him to let you know what had happened, and give you the new number, and I also came here to the house and put a note through the door, giving you the new one. I tried to make sure you got it." He shook his head. "Andrew didn't get the message apparently. I don't know what happened, but he didn't know where you were, or what had happened to you. He didn't even know you were missing until Sam told him yesterday, even though I'd asked him, if he knew where you were. And the note you put through the door was put on my desk by Mrs. Bradley, but it must have been moved, it got caught up in some other papers, and I didn't see it when I came home. But when did you finally get your exam results? Andrew told me that you had to wait for them for a while, and you weren't able to celebrate with your friends, and I hadn't been able to see you at all. I tried to contact you again, on Friday, but had the same problem obviously, and when I finally had time to go to the ward and talk to Sister Eames, she told me she didn't know your results either, and told me that you'd had your purse stolen, but didn't mention your phone. What happened?"

Francesca told him the whole story, interrupted by the entry of Mrs. Bradley with a tray of coffee, who didn't stay, just put the tray down, before she went back to the kitchen. When she had gone, and Dominic was holding her close, Francesca found she was feeling better. His reaction to the story was everything she could have asked for, and he held her close, as he kissed her again. "Oh you poor darling" he said "It's been a very difficult time for you, hasn't it? I was hoping to be able to take you out for dinner, and couldn't, and then you got told that you had to move out of the nurses home. I'd have never allowed that to happen, I'd have bought you back here immediately. I love you so very much, and I've been so bad tempered while I couldn't talk to you, and be with you."

"You love me?" she asked, and he nodded. "I've loved you from the first time I saw you, when you bumped into me when you were going back to the nurses home, after you'd been shopping, and when you agreed to go out with me, I just wanted to hold you close, and never let you go."

"Oh Dominic" she sighed, "I love you too, and when I thought you didn't want to see me again, I was so

unhappy."
"I'm never going to let you be unhappy again." he said as he kissed her, "Marry me please sweetheart?" and he held her close, as he kissed her again.
"Oh yes Dominic" she sighed when he lifted his head, "yes I will." and she was kissed again, for her pains. He held her close as he said, "I want you to be part of my life as soon as we can manage it, unless of course you want a big wedding with loads of bridesmaids and thousands of guests."
"No," she said, "I just want a quiet wedding, just you and me, and our witnesses."
"I'm so glad you said that." he said quietly, "I'll get a special licence and we can be married within a week."
"So soon" she asked, and he smiled. "We have no reason to wait, do we?" he asked, and she shook her head. "No." she said. "No reason at all." He held her close, kissed her again and again, and she wondered what her friends and family would say when they found out her news. The housekeeper knocked on the door then, and when she came in, Dominic told her they would be dining out that evening. She had smiled at them both. "Celebrating your return, are you?" she asked, and he had nodded, but when she had gone out of the room, Francesca smiled at him. "You're going to have to tell her the news" she said, and he nodded, before he kissed her again. They told Mrs. Bradley they were to be married, but swore her to secrecy, and the housekeeper had gone home that evening, happy at their news. "I'm going to take you out for dinner" Dominic announced "just to celebrate your exam

results, and our engagement." She nodded but looked worried, "I haven't got that many clothes with me. I don't want to show you up"
"You'll never do that" he said, "do you have that chestnut coloured one with you?" and when she nodded, said, "wear that one. It suits you so well, and I'd like to see it on you. "She smiled at him. "Can I take my case upstairs and sort it out?" she asked, and he shook his head. "No, I'll take it for you, and you can decide where you want to sleep. I've done up a couple of the bedrooms, so you can take your pick." He led her upstairs, and showed her the room she had always had when she lived there. It was different, but she couldn't work out what was missing, until he said, "We demolished the cupboard that was in the corner, and it's now got wardrobes in there instead. Do you want to use this one?" She nodded, and he smiled at her. "Until after we are married," he said, and then laughed at the expression on her face. She blushed, and he laughed even more, before leaving her alone. She swiftly unpacked her case, found the dress, and put it on, did her hair and face, and went back downstairs again, where he was waiting for her, a small parcel in his hands. "I was going to give you this when we first found it." he said. "But you'd gone and I wasn't able to. We found it, and I think it's probably yours." Puzzled, she opened the parcel, and then an expression of joy spread over her face, as she looked at the toy stuffed rabbit it contained. "This is Jiminy Bunny" she said. "My father bought him for me when I was about two. I was going to call him Jimmy Bunny, but I mispronounced it, and he became Jiminy

instead. I had him until I was about five. I kept him in the toy cupboard in the bedroom, and I would put him on a shelf at night, because I had to put all my toys away. One night, I put him away, then the next morning, I couldn't find him. Mum and Dad searched high and low for him, but we never found him, and I remember crying because he'd gone. Dad told me he'd gone to find somewhere else to live, and I believed him. Where was he?"

"There was a small gap between the shelves and the board at the back of the cupboard, and he must have fallen down there. I'm not surprised your father wasn't able to find him. He would have needed to take the cupboard apart, to find him."

"Oh Dominic, thank you for finding him, and returning him to me. He's a special toy for me." She leant up and kissed him, and was caught and held close, as he returned the caress. "We'll keep him for our children, shall we?" he asked, "And incidentally, how many do you want?"

"I don't mind, but not quite a cricket team." He smiled, and picked up her coat, helping her on with it. "Come on then, I'm going to take you out to celebrate. I've got to work tomorrow I'm afraid, but I can be free the day after that, so I'll start making enquiries about a special licence. We could be married next week, if that would be okay?" She smiled, as she envisaged becoming his wife, and knew they would be happy together.

The next few days passed in a whirl of activity. Dominic had arranged a special licence for their marriage for his next free day, which was the Friday of that week, and she had spent an enjoyable day shopping for a dress to wear, and also shopping with Dominic for an engagement ring and their wedding rings. "Are we going to invite your sister and brother?" he asked but she shook her head. "Would you mind if we just kept everything quiet for a while?" she asked. "Everybody, including Sam and Andy, are going to think that we're being too hasty, getting married literally eight weeks after we met, so if we just kept on going out together occasionally, we could have a honeymoon, in about three or four months' time, and nobody need know that we've been married already. Also, I don't really want my sister-in-law to be at our wedding. I don't think she likes me too much, and I'm sure she wiped the message giving my new phone number from their answer machine, without telling Andy that I'd left it, and she'd probably be very scathing about the fact that you are marrying me. Given that you're a consultant and Andy's boss to boot." He had smiled at her vehemence, and agreed to their having a very private, secret wedding day. They were relaxing at home in the evening, after a long day at work for Dominic, and she was cuddled up to him, as he held her close to him. He bent his head, to kiss her again and again, and their positions subtly altered, so he was lying almost on top of her. His hands were gently stroking her breasts, through her blouse, and she gasped, as sensations she had never felt before, went through her body. "Do you like that?" he asked and she nodded. "Am I rushing you?" he asked, as he kissed her again, but she shook her head. "No" she said, "We're going to be married in two days time, so you aren't rushing me at all. I'm just worried I won't know what to do." He grinned at her, "You won't need to do anything" he said. "Oh Francesca, I love you so much, and I hope you'll enjoy me making love to you," and he kissed her again. "I think I shall" she said. "When you've been kissing me, and you stop and go away, I feel lost." Dominic kissed her again. "I'll never stop kissing you my darling, and I'll never go away from you" he said, and bent his head again. He was caressing her body as he kissed her, and this time, he didn't stop for a long time, and when he finally lifted his head, she was smiling, a smile that he looked at with satisfaction. "Shall we go upstairs?" he asked, and she nodded. "If you're going to make me feel like that again, I don't care where we go" she replied, and he smiled at her words. He stood up and pulled her to her feet, and led her up the staircase to his bedroom.

Francesca lay back against the pillows, and watched as Dominic came towards her, holding a bottle of wine and a couple of glasses. She was tired, but very happy, and hadn't realised that she could feel the way she did. Dominic smiled at her, as he set the glasses and bottle down on the bedside table, and came to sit beside her. "Are you okay?" he asked and she smiled as she said "Definitely. Did you know you could make me feel like that?" He nodded, "I hoped I could" he said, as he poured out a couple of glasses of wine, and handed one to her. "Drink that, my darling" he said softly, and she placed the glass on the bedside table, before he bent his head to kiss her softly. When he lifted his head, and she

was able to take a drink of the liquid, she looked up at him. "I'd better make an appointment to go and see the family planning clinic, hadn't I?" she said. "That way, I'll be responsible, won't I?"
"You don't have to if you don't want to" he smiled at her, "but that's going to be your decision and I'll abide by anything you decide. Now, lay back and drink your wine." and he took a sip of his own drink, before he put the glass down on the bedside table, and he kissed her again. It was much later, when he pulled her head onto his shoulder, and told her to close her eyes. "If I'm not here when you wake up, I'll be back as soon as I can" he said, as he kissed her again. "Mrs. Bradley will be in about 9.00 am, as usual, and she'll make you your breakfast. Eat something, because you've lost weight and it doesn't suit you." he smiled as she closed her eyes, and he gently kissed her goodnight, held her close, and watched as she slipped into a deep relaxing sleep.

Two days later, they stood in front of the registrar, who had inspected the paperwork, and birth certificates, before he started the ceremony. Ten minutes later, the deed was done, and they were man and wife, their witnesses having been two people who had been waiting for their chance to get married, and as they stood together outside the hall, he bent down and kissed her. "Hello Mrs. Cavanagh" he said softly. "Where shall we go for our honeymoon?" She laughed, for he was due to be on call all weekend, and she was to start work on Monday, in the Theatre Unit. He held her hand, as they went down the stairs to the street, and walked slowly back to where the Bentley was parked. They were walking along the street, his arm was around her shoulders, as they walked, and he bent his head to kiss her. They didn't know they were being watched. Maggie Lewis, the Sister in charge of the Theatre Unit, had fallen for Dominic in a big way, and she gave the impression that she considered him to be her property. She knew that Francesca was going to be starting work in Theatres in a couple of days time, and she watched the girl, laughing up at something that Dominic said, and her jealousy came to the forefront. She determined there and then, that Francesca would be kept away from Dominic at all costs, and they would never be able to work together. She sighed, and went to have a coffee and take some tablets for the ever-present headache that was keeping her awake at nights, then went on duty in the Theatre Unit that afternoon, and altered the off duty so that Dominic's on call nights did not match Francesca's late duties. She hadn't seen the wedding rings they both wore, and still hoped that Dominic would show some interest in her, despite the difference in their ages. He was on call over the weekend, and she always put herself on duty when he was due to work. Dominic had noticed the way she acted towards him, but he had never given her any indication that he felt as she did, and he had laughed about it with Francesca, but he did not realise how deep her feelings were, something which could cause problems in the future.

He wasn't required to go into theatres over the weekend, for Andrew was able to deal with any emergencies, and was able to spend the time with Francesca, as they started their married life together, and it was on the Sunday evening, as they sat together over their meal, that Francesca began to worry about whether anything would be said. "What am I going to say if Ally asks me why I've moved out?" she asked, and Dominic laughed. "Just say that you decided to get yourself somewhere to live, where you aren't going to be asked to move, at a moment's notice. She was really upset you were told to move, wasn't she?" She smiled, and nodded. "I'll go and see Samantha soon. I saw her a couple of days ago, but only for a few minutes, and she's been leaving messages, asking me for a meal, and I've got to tell her about what happened. I want to tell her about you and I, but I'll put that off for a while, I think." Dominic agreed, "When you decide to tell her, invite her here for a meal, and we can tell her then." he grinned, "I reckon she will want to know why are living with me, and will want to know what my intentions towards you are." She smiled and continued. "Are you going to carry on wearing your ring?" she asked, "I'm going to have to leave mine off completely, and as Sister Lewis is always so hot on hospital rules, I won't be able to wear it on a chain round my neck. Where do you reckon she'll put me to work? When I went for my interview, she told me I might stay in General Theatres for a while, but when I was on a late duty, I might be required to work in any of the other theatres, so I would have to work in those occasionally. You never know, I might get to work with you."

"I'd be good to you, if you do work with me, and to

answer your question, I'm not going to wear the ring at work. That would give everything away." he said. "Actually, I've just thought about something. Every time I do an on call, Maggie Lewis works a late duty, or she works the weekend, if I'm on call then. I bet she worked this weekend." he kissed her gently, "I won't see you very often if you are working in General Theatre, but at least we'll be able to spend the evenings together, and we can have some weekends together." He cuddled her close, and kissed her. "I'd better go and do some sandwiches for tomorrow's lunch" she said, as she sat up, and he let her go. "I'll be back soon" she rose from her seat and went out to the kitchen. She was buttering bread, when he came into the kitchen, and kissed the back of her neck. "If you do that, I'll be longer than you want me to be." she said, but she turned in his arms, and he kissed her. When he lifted his mouth from hers, she grinned. "For goodness sake, don't think about doing that at work" she said. "It might cause a bit of a sensation."
"It would be a good way of telling everybody we were married" he said, and smiled. "Finish making your sandwich, and then let's go to bed. I've just phoned Andrew, he says there's nothing come in that I might be needed for, so we should be okay." She grinned, made the sandwich, and wrapped it up, then put it into the fridge. "Don't let me forget it" she said, and watched as he locked the doors, turned the lights up, and then took her hand and led her up to bed.

The following day, he took her back to the nurses

home, and she opened the door of her new room, and found her luggage all ready to unpack. She didn't unpack anything, as she wouldn't be using the room, using it instead as an address for mail to be sent to, for she would be going home to be with Dominic each evening. He had worried about her walking back to the house when she was on a late duty, but she had laughed at him, for she had always walked to and fro, when she had been living with her mother, but it felt nice to be cared for. She had arranged for Dan to come and pick her up that evening, to collect her luggage, and take it to Dominic's house, and hoped that none of her friends would see her moving, for they would want to know where she was going, but as the ward hours were different to theatre hours, she didn't think that anybody would notice. She wasn't going to be wearing uniform any more, unless it was at an official occasion, so she was dressed in casual clothes and apprehensively went to the theatre unit. She was greeted by Sister Lewis, told to get dressed into theatre wear, and come back to see her. She had worked in the unit as a student, so she knew where everything was in the department, so she didn't feel too strange, but Sister Lewis's attitude had subtly altered since she was a student. She didn't know what she had done, but it didn't seem as if she was too welcome. She shrugged off the feeling, and listened to what the other woman was saying. She was given her off duty, told she would be working in General Theatres, and would not be going to work in any other theatre for a while as Sister wanted her to become adept at general surgery, before she went to any other theatre. As she looked at the off duty, she realised she was on completely opposite duties to Dominic. She was on an early duty when he was on call, and her weekends on duty were when he was off. Still, she consoled herself, she would be able to spend some time with him when she wasn't on duty, and went with Sister to find one of the staff nurses who would be her mentor.

She enjoyed her first day at work, and that evening, she made her way home to their house. Mrs. Bradley told her that Dominic would be home later that evening, and Francesca wondered what he was doing at that moment. He wasn't thinking about her at that moment – he was busy, working on a young boy's leg, trying with all his considerable skill, to save it. Andrew was helping him along with the senior house officer, and the scrub nurse was Sister Lewis. At length, Dominic managed to repair the artery that had been torn away during the accident, and which had caused him such concern. "I think we've done it" he announced, and smiled at the people gathered around the table. "I'll just get the plate into position, then we can finish up. Thanks for your assistance, everybody." he said, and straightened his back. "I'll finish up, if you want me to" Andrew said, but Dominic shook his head. "No, thanks Andrew. I'll put the last few screws into this plate, then we can sew up, and do a quick round of the patients before I go home."
"Doing anything special this evening?" asked the anaesthetist, but Dominic shook his head. "Nothing much" he announced. "Got to clear up some

paperwork, so I'll get that done tonight" he held out his hand, and Sister Lewis put the needle holder into it. "Thanks Sister" he said quietly. "You always know exactly what I need." he was referring to the instruments he used during the surgery, but the woman took his comments the wrong way, and glowed with pride, as she imagined spending more time with him. "Do you have any news of the nurses who are going to start here?" he asked her, and she nodded. "Well, one of them started today. She's not much good at the moment, so I've put her to work in General Theatres. I'll keep her there, until she's got more experience, before she begins to work in the other theatres."
"Any more going to start?" he asked, but she shook her head. "Nobody at the moment, but I'm always hopeful" she said, then looked across to her runner nurse. "Final swab count, Nurse" she demanded, and when it was completed, "Swabs, needles and instruments are correct Mr. Cavanagh" she announced, and then watched as the surgeons asked for the plaster trolley to be bought in. "Give the surgeons some assistance Nurse Evans, and then you can stock up the implants. Make sure you do the ordering tonight." she ordered, as she pushed her trolleys into the sluice to dispose of her instruments, and her staff breathed a sigh of relief as she went.
"She doesn't trust you, does she?" the auxiliary asked the staff nurse, as the door shut behind her.
"No, and I'm getting fed up with it. She was off duty at 5.00 but she won't go if Mr. C. has got a case to finish. She considers him, her private property, and it would be quite funny, if it wasn't so tragic." she

stopped talking as Sister came back into the room, and went to make sure her paperwork was in order. Dominic was washing his hands, having shed his gown and gloves, before going to write up the notes, when Sister Lewis went to stand beside him at the row of sinks, and started to wash hers as well.
“Thanks for your help, Sister” he said again, “Weren't you meant to be off duty at 5.00?”
“Yes,” she said, “but I'm not doing anything this evening, and it seemed sensible to stay and finish the case, as I was here and scrubbed already.”
“You didn't have to do that Sister” he said quietly, “I appreciate it, obviously, but you shouldn't stay when there's no need.”
“I don't mind” she said, “but I'll go home now. Good evening, Mr. Cavanagh” and she left the theatre, to hand over the patient to the recovery nurses. When she had gone, there was a very different atmosphere in the theatre, and Andrew, who was assisting the nurses to clear up, looked up from his task. “I wish she wouldn't stay on all the time, when you're operating Dominic” he said, “She puts herself on duty when you're on call, and won't let anybody else scrub for any operation you want to scrub for.” Dominic nodded. “I'd noticed that” he said, “Was she on duty this weekend?” Andrew nodded “She was a bit miffed because I didn't need to call you in.” he said, then grinned, “Have you noticed, she only ever puts the married nurses in here, to assist her? She's keeping the unmarried ones away from you. I think she fancies you.” Dominic was startled at his registrar's words, but he said nothing, just looked questioningly at the younger man. “You're joking?”

he said eventually, but Andrew nodded. “I think everybody has noticed it” he said, and Stephanie Evans nodded. “Honestly it's true.” she said. “She won't let anybody who is unmarried in here with you, in case you fall for her. We've all noticed it. And God help anybody who you go out with. Maggie Lewis has got a bit of a nasty streak in her at the moment, and if she saw you with anybody else, then I wouldn't like to be in that person's shoes, if she were unlucky enough to have to work with her.” Dominic was silent for a moment. “What would happen if I got married?” he asked, and Stephanie laughed. “I don't think your wife's life would be worth living, if she found out about it. Are you thinking of getting married?” she asked, and smiled. “If so, who are you marrying?” She grinned at him. “Excuse me being so nosy, but we're always interested in the private lives of our surgeons.”
He smiled back at her. “Nobody at the moment” he said eventually, “but when I do, I'll let you know who the lucky woman will be.”
“Oh good, you'll have to bring her here and show her off. But please let me know when you're intending to do it, because I really want to see Maggie Lewis's face when you announce that you're getting married. I know that sounds nasty, but we've put up with her for a long time, and now she's decided that she fancies you, and she's made you her property. I think she’s a bit obsessed with you. She's always been a bit odd, but it’s got a lot worse lately.” Dominic looked startled, then grinned. “I'll have to start looking for somebody” he said. “Thanks for telling me.” He finished writing, then handed Andrew the notes. “I'll

go and get changed; we can do a quick round then I'll be off" he said. "See you tomorrow, everybody. Thanks for your help girls" then he left the theatres and went to the changing room.

As he drove home, later than he had planned, he decided to tell Francesca what Stephanie had said about Sister Lewis. He didn't understand why she had become fixated on him; she was over 20 years older than he was, and then he thought about the comments about him marrying, and how the nurses were speculating about him being seen with another woman. He smiled as he garaged the car, and went into the house, where Francesca was waiting for him. He opened his arms and she flew into them, and as he hugged her close, and kissed her soundly, he hoped there would not be any trouble for her in the future.

Chapter Seven

"For goodness sake Staff Nurse Hallett, concentrate on what you are doing" Sister Lewis snapped at Francesca, as she failed to hand the instrument to the surgeon she was assisting, before he asked her for it. Francesca blushed under her mask. She had been scrubbing for the surgeons for the last five weeks, and she felt she was doing well, but whenever Sister Lewis entered the theatre, she became unsure of her actions, and knew that the other woman didn't like her, and had wondered why. Now, she handed the instrument to the surgeon, and didn't look up, and heard the door close, and knew without anybody saying so, that the older woman had left the room. "She really doesn't like you, does she?" said the surgeon, and Francesca nodded.
"She's been like that since I came here, but she was so glad that I wanted to work here when I went for the interview. She told the nursing officer that I would be very welcome, and she couldn't wait for me to arrive."
"Well, don't worry Fran, you're doing very well, for somebody who's only been here for a few weeks, you've managed to learn very quickly. As you get more experience, you'll be doing the more complicated cases, and she won't be able to say anything derogatory about you."
"She's probably frustrated" said the anaesthetist, and everybody laughed, as he continued. "Seriously, I bet she is. She's got it into her head, that she fancies one of the Orthopods, won't let anybody else scrub for him, stays late whenever his cases run over,

and every on call he does, she does a late duty. She always does the weekends when he's on call as well. I feel sorry for him."

"Who is it?" demanded Mr. Leigh, the surgeon who Fran was scrubbed for, and the anaesthetist grinned. "It's Dominic Cavanagh, the new Orthopaedic surgeon" he announced "It's very noticeable. I've been doing his lists recently, and she always scrubs for him. Poor sod, he didn't realise what she was doing, until a few weeks ago, when his list over ran quite late and she stayed on to finish it with him. She finally went home, and left Steph Evans to clear up after her, and it was she who told him, that they all felt sorry for anybody who he went out with. They all reckon that Maggie Lewis would give the girl hell, if she saw them together, and the girl came to work in theatres, or even visit him here. He didn't say anything, just said he'd have to start looking for somebody to marry, to put Maggie off, but he looked very thoughtful." Both men laughed together, but nothing else was said, as they continued with the case. Fran finished the case and started to clear up after herself, but as she went into the sluice with the trolley, she remembered what had been said, and knew now the reason why Sister Lewis was acting the way she did towards her. She must have seen them together, she realised, and this was her revenge. But what she didn't know was that they were married already, and nothing was going to be able to interfere with that. She was enjoying her new work, and it was only the attitude of Sister Lewis that was upsetting it. She sighed, and went back into the theatre, to help the Staff Nurse get ready for the next case. As she opened packets of swabs, and counted them with the girl, she wondered what would happen, when they finally did announce that they were married.

That evening, Dominic was on call, and he was delayed in theatres. He had managed to phone her, and let her know he would be late, so she ate the meal that Mrs. Bradley had supplied, and went to the sitting room to relax, turned the television on, and curled up on the settee. She had spent an evening with her sister a couple of weeks before, but hadn't told her anything about being with Dominic, and knew it was getting more difficult to hide her relationship with him, and wondered if they should announce it. Her phone rang, and she went to answer it. "Fran, it's Andy" a voice announced. "I haven't seen you for ages, even though we work in the same area. I wondered how you were?"
"I'm fine" she said. "How are you and how's Theresa?" They exchanged news for a couple of minutes, then Andy said, "I was wondering whether you'd like to come for a meal in a couple of days. Theresa was saying she hadn't seen you or Sam for a while, so we could all get together. But I wanted to know, are you still seeing Dominic? Sam told me that you and he were together, when you went away, after your results, when he couldn't contact you, and he asked me for news, asking if I'd heard from you, and he sounded really worried about you. When Sam finally got your new number and gave it to me to give to him, he changed from being bad tempered to somebody quite different. Are you

and he an item? If so, we could all get together and have a meal. We probably won't be able to do that once the baby arrives, so we should make every effort now."

"Yes, I'm still seeing Dominic. But Andy, for heaven's sake, don't mention it at the hospital." she answered with a smile. "I'd love to see you and Theresa and Sam again. When are you thinking of inviting everybody?"

"Well, I know he's not on call on Thursday, and if I read the off duty correctly, you're not working. How about Thursday evening? I've spoken to Sam and she's not working that day. Come about 7.00 and we can all have a talk together before the meal."

"Okay" she said. "Dominic and I were due to meet then anyway. It's about the only day this week, that we're both off together."

"Yes," he said dryly, "I had noticed. We'll talk about that when we get together." He laughed, and they continued talking about what they had been doing since they last saw each other. They were on the phone for a long time, before Andrew said "Okay Fran, I'll see you Thursday" and he disconnected. Francesca sat back against the cushions, and thought about things. If other people had noticed the disparity in their off duty, then surely something would have to be done about it. She decided to talk to Dominic about whether or not she should tell her brother and sister about their relationship, and yawned, before turning her attention back to the television and the programme she had been watching.

She had spent the rest of the evening alone, had a long bath and finally, gone to bed, and was reading, when the front door opened, and she knew Dominic was home. He came upstairs and greeted her, and sat tiredly on the bed beside her. “Was it bad?” she asked and he nodded. “There was a pile up on the motorway, and we had to call in another team and open another theatre. We'd been trying to get hold of Andrew, but he was on the phone, and we couldn't get him, for quite a while.”
“He was talking to me” she said, “Did you manage to get hold of him okay?” Dominic nodded. “Yes, we got through eventually. He's in now and working, and I came home, just to make sure that you're okay. I couldn't talk on the phone in the department, because there are too many people around including Maggie Lewis, who decided to stay, and is now getting completely in the way of everybody. When I announced I was going to come home for a while, she decided to go off duty, so I won't have to work with her when I get back. I've got to go back in, because we've got a very nasty pelvis to work on, but the patient has also got internal injuries, so while the general surgeons were doing their stuff, I decided to see how you were.” He kissed her gently, and she responded. “I'm fine” she said. “I wondered what was happening, but now I know, I'm fine. Go back, go and save the patient with the pelvis, and I'll see you tomorrow evening. I'm on a late duty, but I'll see you when I can.” He kissed her again. “What an understanding wife I've got” he said, as he got up, then bent and kissed her again. “Sleep well, my darling. I'll phone you tomorrow

evening." and he left the room, and she heard the front door close behind him. She smiled to herself. He was obviously very busy, but he had made enough time to come and see how she was and she loved him more than ever, for his thoughtfulness. She made sure the alarm was set, turned the lights out, and tried to sleep, something which she found it hard to do.

The following day, she was due to do a late duty, but went to the nurses home first, to see if there was any post, and found several letters waiting for her. There was a hand written note from her sister, which she read swiftly. "Where the hell are you?" she read. "Every time I phone, it goes straight to voicemail, you never answer any messages I leave for you with Maggie Lewis in theatre, you're never in your room, and your neighbours say you don't seem to live here anymore. Fran, what's happened? Phone me urgently please." She smiled to herself and knew she owed her sister a very big explanation, but she'd not been able to contact Sam since their evening together, knew she ought to have tried to do something about it before, and knew she and Dominic would have to admit that they were living together. She went to the internal phone and got through to the ward. Luckily the call wasn't answered by her sister, and she left a message, telling her that she was okay, but she'd explain everything when she saw her at their brother's house on the following day, and replaced the receiver, thankful that she hadn't had to speak to her, but she would have Dominic with her when she did finally see her sister.

She was walking towards the coffee room that afternoon for her tea break before she scrubbed for a case, when she heard her brother's voice in the corridor, and looked round the corner. He had come into the main body of the theatres, and was standing talking to Sister Lewis, and she could hear everything that was being said. "Sorry to bother you Sister" he said now, "I was wondering if I could have a word with my sister, Staff Nurse Hallett."
"Your sister?" Maggie Lewis said, "I didn't know she was your sister?"
"Didn't the similarity of the names mean anything?" he asked, but Francesca watched the older woman shake her head. "I'm afraid Staff Nurse Hallett is unavailable at the moment, but I can give her a message from you" she said. Francesca's initial reaction was to go and see what her brother wanted, but decided against it. Sister Lewis was in a bad enough mood as it was, for she had been forced to go off duty yesterday evening, and one of the night staff nurses had taken over from her, so she hadn't been able to scrub for Dominic for all of the cases. The other girls had laughed about it, but it had been noticeable that her temper was very bad today.
"Okay" Andy said, "could you tell Fran, that Mr. Cavanagh has said he'll give her a lift to my house tomorrow evening, so could she be ready when he comes to collect her at 6.45 from outside the nurses home. We're having a meal together with my other sister and some friends." he explained, and Sister Lewis nodded. "I'll pass the message on." she said,

and watched as Andy left the department. Francesca walked into the coffee room, and made herself a drink. This was her tea break, and she felt she needed it. Sister Lewis walked into the room, and stared at her. "What are you doing?" she asked. "Who told you to have a drink?"
"Staff Nurse Evans told me to have my break now" she answered. "She wants me to scrub for Mr. Davenport's last case, and told me to have a drink before it starts." She waited for the older woman to give her, her brother's message, but it wasn't forthcoming, and she knew that it wouldn't be passed on. "Well, don't take longer than 15 minutes" she was told, and finally she was left alone. She knew she was entitled to a 30-minute break, but couldn't be bothered to argue, and sat and drank the tea before washing her cup, and going back to the theatre, wondering what she could do, for Sister Lewis was making her life very uncomfortable lately.

That evening, she was able to phone Dominic, when Sister and the early staff had gone home, and she was in private. "Has Andrew told you he's invited us to dinner tomorrow night?" she asked, then realised he must have done. "Sorry, stupid of me, when you told him to tell me that you'd give me a lift. I think we're going to have to tell them." She spoke. "I've had a note from Sam, asking me where the hell I'm living now, and I can't lie to them forever. We've had a few weeks on our own now, so I think it's about time, don't you?"
"Yes, probably be a good idea" he said softly, "You're tired, aren't you?" he asked.

"I was worried about you last night" she said, "so I didn't sleep too well. But what about you? What time did you finish operating? Nobody here knows."
"We finished the pelvis about 3.00 a.m., but then I had to work on a badly fractured femur, so we were still operating until about 7.00 this morning. Then I had to do a ward round, so I finally got home after you'd left. Mrs. Bradley told me you'd been gone about 30 minutes before I opened the front door. I've slept all afternoon, and I'll be coming back to pick you up this evening." he sighed "I missed you last night, and that bed was very cold and lonely this afternoon."
"I know what you mean." she said, as she smiled. "It was lonely last night as well. I've got to go, my darling, I'm only having a ten minute break, but I'll see you tonight. Same place as always?" she asked, and was assured it would be. "I'll see you soon" he said, "Take care, won't you?"
She said her farewells, put the phone back in her locker, and went back to the office. Annie Ford was there, and she looked up as Francesca went back into the room. "Been talking to the boyfriend?" she asked. "You've got a very satisfied look on your face." she joked, and Francesca nodded. "Wanted to make sure of something" she said, and turned her attention to what Annie was telling her. It was as they were changing, ready to go home, that Annie spoke again. "Fran, is Sister Lewis getting to you? We've all noticed that she seems to have it in for you, and nobody can work out why. What on earth have you done to make her dislike you so much?"
"I don't know" Francesca said, aware that she wasn't

going to tell anybody the truth for a while. "She was always so nice to me when I was a student, said she was looking forward to me coming back to work here at my interview, but in the intervening weeks, she's changed. If I can keep out of her way, and do my job properly, then perhaps she'll alter her opinion."

"I don't think she's very well. She told me she's been having a lot of very bad headaches lately, but she won't go and see anybody about them." confided Annie. "We all know she's got a thing for Mr. Cavanagh, always scrubs for his list whenever he's doing one, always does the weekends, when he's on call, and is generally sickening to watch, whenever he's around, but she's never acted as she has to anybody else who came to work here, as she's doing to you," she grinned impishly at Francesca "You haven't got friendly with Mr. C., have you? That's the only thing I can think of that might have influenced her feelings."

Francesca shook her head. "I never see him in the theatres. I'm not allowed into the Orthopaedic Theatres, if you remember. He only ever says hello to me, if we pass in the corridor" she said, crossing her fingers as she told the untruth. "He did take me out once or twice when I was working as a student, because his father was a patient of mine, and he had a major cardiac event, and I had to do CPR before the team arrived, and he wanted to say thank you, but we haven't been out for ages, certainly since before my results came through." Annie nodded. "Perhaps she saw you with him, and got the wrong impression" she said. "But I thought I'd tell you to watch out." she smiled at Francesca. "We'll all try and help as much as we can, but when she gets an idea in her head, it's difficult to change it for her." she sighed. "Anyway, go off duty, and I'll see you tomorrow. Have a good evening – what's left of it anyway." and she watched as Francesca walked out of the department.

Dominic was waiting for her, away from the main gate of the hospital, and as she got into the car, he leant forward and kissed her. "Were you busy?" he asked her, but she shook her head. "No, not really" she said. "The list finished about six, and after that, we just cleared up, got everything ready for tomorrow, and Annie Ford gave me a teaching session on some of the other instruments I might be dealing with, eventually, if Maggie Lewis ever lets me out of General Theatres." she grinned, but Dominic couldn't see her, as he was concentrating on the road ahead. "She started with the Orthopaedic instruments, and it made me think, you're not really a surgeon, are you? You're a carpenter."
"I'll give you a carpenter" he growled, but he was grinning. They had gone into the house now, and he took her in his arms and held her close, as he kissed her. "Did you get the message that Andrew gave Maggie Lewis?" he asked, "I sent that deliberately, because I wanted to see if you'd get it. She's not passing on quite a few messages apparently. I overheard your sister telling one of her friends that you never answer the messages she leaves with Maggie, for you to phone her, and she's been getting a bit worried." Francesca shook her head. "I heard

Andrew giving it to her, but she didn't give it to me, even though I was only in the coffee room, but I got a message from Sam, which she left in my room at the home, asking me why I never phone her back, when she leaves messages with Maggie Lewis for me to do so."
"I didn't think she'd pass it on" he said, "I'll make certain that I never leave a message with her if I need to get something to you urgently. I shouldn't have to, because I'll be able to see you. Now, what you said about telling everybody tomorrow. I think I agree with you. I think your sister and brother need to know, and I'm going to enjoy seeing their faces when we tell them. We'll have to wear our rings obviously."
"It will be nice to think that they will know that we're married." she smiled at him, and reached up to kiss him. "I've got a bottle of wine here" he said, "Come on, I'll pour you a drink." and he led her into the sitting room.

On the following day, she had gone into work on an early duty, and she was helping Steph to lay up for an operation, when Sister Lewis came into the theatre to see her. "Nurse Hallett" she began, "We have a problem with shortage of staff. There is going to be a severe shortage of people this evening, so I will require you to change duties. You will work a split shift today. You will go off duty at mid-day and return to duty at 5.00pm."
"No" she said, "I can't. I have an engagement this evening. I'm sorry Sister, but I cannot change shifts."
"I'm not giving you any option" Sister Lewis said

angrily. "I am the senior Sister in this department, and I am telling you, you will work this evening. Your engagement will have to be cancelled."
"I cannot cancel the engagement." she said angry now, and knowing that the woman was trying to stop her from seeing Dominic. "You won't allow me to see my brother when I'm working, because I'm not allowed in the Orthopaedic theatres, I can't see my sister because she's working on the wards, and tonight is the only time we've been able to arrange a time when we can all get together, when we're not on duty. I don't see them very often, and there are other people invited as well apparently. Why can't you find somebody else to do the duty?"
"I am not going to explain my actions to you." Sister Lewis said. "Go off duty at 12.00 as I told you, and report back here at 5.00 pm. If you do not return, then you need not come back to work, because I will have you replaced."
"Who with?" Francesca argued angrily, "You can't get any more staff anyway. If I go, then you'll be really short of staff."
"Don't argue Staff Nurse." Sister Lewis said, as she turned away, "Make sure you return by 5.00 p.m."
Francesca watched her go, and knew she would have to try and contact Dominic and Andy urgently. She walked into the changing room, opened her locker and took out her mobile phone. She hurriedly went into the toilet, and locked the door behind her, for that was the only place she could be sure of being private, and dialled Dominic's number. Luckily, he answered swiftly, and she told him what had happened. He swore, as he listened to her story.

She was almost in tears, as she explained everything, and he hurriedly told her not to cry. “Don't worry my darling” he said. “I'll explain to Andrew and Samantha, and I'll tell them about us, but I think from now on, we'll have to make certain that Maggie Lewis knows nothing about any date we might have with anybody else. This proves beyond all doubt that she's trying to split us up. She must have seen us together. She's already failed to pass on a message to you from Andrew, she's not telling you that Samantha wants you to contact her, and now she's changed your off duty, so that you won't be able to go to Andrew's house and have me give you a lift from the hospital, and be alone with you.” Francesca listened to his words. “Oh Dominic, what am I going to do? I love working in theatres, but she's making it impossible for me to learn how to do things.”
“Don't worry sweetheart. Go home at lunchtime, have something to eat, then go back on duty on time. I'll see you this evening, but I think we're going to have to say something to her.”
“Don't say anything yet Dominic” she begged. “We'll have to have a talk, before you say something to her.”
“Okay” he agreed. “I'll see you later on, this evening. I'll pick you up at the usual time, unless you phone me otherwise. I'll miss you. I love you darling.”
“And I love you” she said softly, and disconnected. She went out into the changing room, and replaced the phone in her locker, and went out into the corridor, then into theatre again. “What on earth is going on?” Stephanie Evans asked. “Why on earth

are you being told to do a split duty? There's nobody off sick, we're fully staffed, so why does she need you on duty?"
"It's because I was going to dinner with my brother and sister this evening and a couple of other people, including Mr. Cavanagh. Andy came in yesterday and asked to see me, but she told him I wasn't available, even though I was only in the coffee room, so he left me a message with her, telling me that Mr. Cavanagh would pick me up from outside the nurses home, and asked her to pass it on. I actually heard him telling her and she said she'd pass the message on, but she didn't."
"Hang on, Is Andrew Hallett your brother?" Stephanie asked, and Francesca nodded, "Yes, and Samantha Hallett on Truro Ward is my sister. I thought everybody knew that?"
"No," Steph said, "I didn't. I knew Sam had a sister, but she never told me what your name was, or that you work in the hospital as well. You don't resemble each other, do you? But that doesn't explain why she's making you work?"
"Because she doesn't want me to be given a lift by Mr. Cavanagh. Everybody has said that she's obsessed with him. I'll bet that's what it is." Steph nodded, "That makes sense" she said. "I think we are going to have to look out for you in future. We need to shelter you from her bad tempers."
"Thank you" said Francesca, still annoyed at Sister Lewis' high handedness. "but it doesn't allow me to go and have dinner with Andy and Sam though, does it? I haven't seen Sam to be able to have a long chat with her, since before I got my exam results,

although we've talked on the phone, because our off duty doesn't coincide, and although I've glimpsed Andy in the distance, I haven't had a chance to have a proper talk to him. If you see him, before I get a chance to talk to him, would you please ask him to phone me. I'm not allowed in the Orthopaedic theatres."
"Yes, and now that instruction makes sense as well." Steph said. "I wondered why she gave explicit orders that you weren't to be allowed to work in that theatre. Why doesn't she like you? Does she expect that you will make Mr. C. fall for you?"
"Probably" she gave a hollow laugh, wondering what they would say when they discovered that they were an item. "I'd better scrub for the first case, hadn't I?"
"I don't know if you'd be able to cope with it." Steph said, "but as I'll have to do the rest of the list, perhaps you'd better. I'll be with you at all the time, so you can ask for any help you need. Don't worry Fran, we'll all help you now we know what's happening." She grinned at the younger girl, and Francesca smiled back. "Thank you" she said. "I do appreciate it."

Francesca went off duty at 12.00 and walked slowly home. Mrs. Bradley was present when she entered the house, and looked surprised to see her.
"What on earth are you doing here at this time of day?" she asked. "I thought you and Mr. Dominic were going out to dinner this evening."
"We were" she admitted, "but the Sister on the unit, decided to change my off duty, and she's making me work this evening. She's obsessed with Dominic, and

doesn't want anybody else to have any contact with him. She found out that Dominic was meant to have been giving me a lift to my brother's house this evening, and when she did, she changed my off duty."
"The old bitch" muttered the housekeeper, and Francesca reluctantly smiled. "I quite agree" she said. "She doesn't allow anybody who isn't married, to work in the same theatre as him, she always tries to work the same duties as him, so she's there if he's on call, and insists on scrubbing for every operation with him. He said there's only one other nurse who's ever scrubbed with him, and that was when he was working at night. He doesn't even like her, and he's never shown any interest in her, but she's got this idea that he is her private property. She's at least 20 years older than him as well. It would be funny, if it wasn't so upsetting. My brother asked her to pass on a message to me yesterday, and she didn't do that, and this morning she changed my off duty."
"Is Mr. Dominic going to say anything?" the housekeeper asked, but she shook her head. "I don't know" she admitted. "I asked him not to say anything yet, but he's incredibly angry with her, and he might just retaliate if she riles him badly enough."
"So let me go and get you some lunch" the housekeeper said. "As you won't be having a meal tonight, I'll make you something now, and that will set you up for the evening. You just sit down and I'll be back in a few minutes." She was as good as her word, and Francesca was soon sitting down to a meal. "Maybe you'd better have a rest after lunch" she was told, "you look tired. I expect you were

worried about Mr. Dominic when he had to spend all night at the hospital. I know all about that, he told me yesterday evening, while you were at work. If you go and lie down, I'll make sure I'll wake you up in time to get back to work by 5.00 pm. Have a good sleep, Fran." and Francesca went upstairs to lie down on their bed.

True to her word, Mrs. Bradley woke her with a cup of tea at 4.00, and Francesca prepared for work. She left the house and walked slowly to the hospital, and walked up the stairs, towards the theatre unit. She was on the final staircase, when she came face to face with Miss Elliot, the nursing officer, who had overall responsibility for all the theatre unit. She was a very pleasant woman, and Francesca had always got on well with her. She was known to be fair, and always tried to help the nursing staff, if she could. "This is an odd time to be going on duty" she said now. "Or have you been working all day and forgotten something, Nurse Hallett?" she asked, and Francesca smiled at her. "I was meant to be on an early duty today, but Sister Lewis changed my off duty and put me onto a split duty. So, I'm just coming back on duty."
"Why did she do that?" Miss Elliot asked. "There aren't any nurses off sick today, and there are plenty of staff on duty tonight. I don't like my staff doing split duties, unless it's absolutely necessary. It's not fair on them."
"I don't know why she changed my duty" Francesca said "at least, I've got an idea, but it can't be proved. I was going out tonight as well."

"Where were you going?" she was asked, and Francesca smiled ruefully as she replied, "To see my brother and sister, and a couple of other people. It was a dinner party arranged by my brother. I haven't seen him for a while, even though he works in Orthopaedics, but I'm not allowed in that theatre, so it would have been nice to meet up with him again."
"I can see no reason why you should have to work, and I don't know why you're not being allowed to work in Orthopaedics. You need to know how to do Bone work." Miss Elliot said. "Come with me, and we'll have a look at the off duty. If there are enough staff on duty, then I think we could stretch a point and let you go to your dinner party, and you could make up the time later on." Francesca smiled. "That would be lovely" she said, keeping pace with the nursing officer as she made her way up the final staircase. The Nursing Officer led the way into the office, and looked at the off-duty book. She swiftly counted up numbers and shook her head. "There are plenty of staff on duty, without you having to work as well" she said. "I wonder where Sister Lewis is?" she paused, "Wait here Staff Nurse, I'll see if I can locate Sister Lewis." and she walked out of the office. Francesca was standing by the door, when Maggie Lewis walked out of Theatre One and saw her standing there. "What are you waiting for?" she asked "Go and get changed immediately. You're needed in Theatre Three this evening."
"No, she's not" said Miss Elliot from behind her. "Sister Lewis, I would like to see you in the office now. Staff Nurse Hallett, I think you can be excused. Go off duty now, and come back on duty again

tomorrow. I believe you're on an early duty. I'll speak to you then." Francesca didn't stop to question the other woman, just thanked her and walked out of the office, pulling her phone out as she did so, and hurriedly phoned Dominic. "I've been reprieved" she said. "Miss Elliot saw me walking up to theatre, and asked me where I was going. I told her I'd been put on a split duty, and she didn't think I should have been, so she had a look at the off duty, and told me I could go off duty. I'm back on an early tomorrow."
"That's fantastic news" he said. "I'll see you at home, and if I were you, I'd phone Andy, and tell him that you're able to come after all. I'll be home in about an hour I hope." and she swiftly said her goodbyes, and walked back the way she had come.

Chapter Eight

The dinner party that took place that evening, was an enjoyable one for Francesca. She had phoned Andy, when she got home from the hospital, telling him that she would be able to come after all, and wondered what Miss Elliot had said to Sister Lewis. There was going to be trouble, she thought, and wondered what was going to happen. She shrugged, and went to get ready to go out for the dinner. Her sister-in-law always appeared well dressed, and she wanted to make sure that she matched her, so she had a quick bath, and washed her hair before she changed into a light blue Laura Ashley dress, she had bought a few weeks prior to starting to see Dominic. It was calf length, with a tucked and pleated bodice, and had long sleeves. She had liked it when she had first seen it, and as she looked in the mirror, she realised that it suited her very well. With it, she wore a pair of high heeled sandals, and put a cashmere stole around her shoulders, in case the night should turn cold. She was ready and waiting when Dominic came home from the hospital, and at the sight of him, she smiled brilliantly, and ran into his arms. Their greeting was everything she had wanted, and he held her away to look at her. "Oh, my darling, you look lovely" he said. "Let me go and get changed, and we can go." He kissed her again, then said, "Are you wearing your ring?" She nodded and held out her hand, so he could see the plain gold band he had put there when they married, topped by the sapphire and diamond engagement ring they had bought together. She had redone her hair and make-up when he came downstairs, wearing a beautifully cut grey suit, silk shirt and a dark silk tie, which gave him the air of what he was, a successful young consultant, and he was wearing his wedding ring. "Are you ready?" he asked. "Shall we go and surprise your family?" She nodded and grinned. "I'm looking forward to this" she said. "We can have a chat about everything that is happening at work as well, because Andy knows most of what's gone on, and Sam will be interested." She smiled but she didn't know how Theresa would react, and hoped there wouldn't be any unpleasantness between them. Theresa had been a nurse, before she got married, she would have known and had worked with Sister Lewis, and hoped she would be sympathetic.

Dominic stopped the car outside Andy's house, then bent his head and kissed her. "Ready?" he asked, and she smiled and nodded. She got out, and he took her hand, and led her up the path. They were holding hands, as the front door opened, and Andy looked at them both, with a smile on his face. "So, you are still friends." he stated, and grinned at them both. "Come in, both of you." and he led the way into the front room. Sam and Theresa were sitting together on one of the settees, and they looked up as the two of them entered. "Fran" cried Samantha, and came across to give her sister a hug. "I haven't seen you for ages" she said. "You never answer your phone, and I couldn't get in touch with you in theatres, because you weren't there, or you were scrubbed, but you never phoned back, when I

left you messages." Francesca and Dominic exchanged glances, and Francesca shook her head. "I saw you two or three weeks ago" she said, "but I haven't had any messages since then, and I wouldn't have been scrubbed every time you phoned" she said. "I think there are quite a lot of things that we need to talk to Sister Lewis about. She's been taking the messages and not passing them on. Sorry, Sam."
"So what have you been doing, and where on earth are you living now? Have you found a flat and moved out? You could have told me your new address."
"Sorry Sam" she said again. "There's been a lot going on lately, and I've been incredibly busy."
"Obviously" Samantha said. "But I'm so glad to see you again. And I like that dress. Do a twirl and let's see it." Francesca put her arms out, and twirled, and Samantha nodded, as she stopped. "It's lovely, isn't it Theresa?" Her sister-in-law nodded. "It's nice to see you again Fran" she said "And I take it this is Mr. Cavanagh? Andy, please introduce us." Her husband nodded, and did the introductions. "Can I get you a drink?" he asked, and turned back to the table where the drinks were set out. Francesca had sat down with her sister now, and was telling her about her work, and soon everybody was listening, as she told her about the problems she was having. Dominic was sitting in an armchair next to her, listening, but when Francesca mentioned that Sister Lewis was being so unpleasant to her, Sam shook her head. "She was never like that when I first knew her" she said. "You knew her as well didn't you Theresa?" Her sister-in-law nodded. "She was the junior sister in theatres when I worked with her, and she got

promotion to Senior Sister a couple of years ago. I left about six months after she got promoted. She was always fair to the students and the other nurses. She sounds as if she's changed radically since I knew her."

"That's another thing" Samantha said, "Stephanie Evans told me last week, she'd been given promotion and was the junior sister in the department, but everybody refers to her as Staff Nurse. Isn't she being allowed to act as a Sister?" Francesca shook her head. "I didn't even know she was a Sister. Nobody ever calls her that." Dominic shook his head. "I didn't know that either" he said.

"But why has she taken against you so much?" Samantha wanted to know, and Francesca knew this was her opportunity. "I believe it's because she saw Dominic and I together, and as she wants him for herself, so she's doing everything to make sure that I don't have any opportunity to see him. She's put me on opposite duties to him, and when Andy asked her to give me a message telling me that Dominic would pick me up tonight, she obviously didn't want me to spend any time alone, in his company, so she didn't pass on the message. And this morning, she told me that she was very short of nurses, and I'd have to do a split duty. It was only the fact that Miss Elliot saw me when I was coming back on duty, and told me that there were enough staff, that she got involved. And that is the reason there was so much confusion about me being able to come tonight."

"But Maggie Lewis is in her mid-50's" Sam said. "She's at least 20 years older than Dominic." Theresa grinned at them both. "Maybe she's after a toy boy

to look after her as she gets older." Everybody laughed at that comment, and Sam looked at her sister. "Are you and Dominic able to spend any time together?" Sam asked, "if she puts you on earlies, when he's on call, and opposite weekends, you aren't able to have much time together."
"Oh, we manage" Dominic said with a smile. "She's waiting for me when I get home, or vice versa, and that's very nice."
"You're living together?" Samantha asked, with an odd expression on her face, and Dominic smiled at her. "Well, husbands and wives do live together, don't they?" he asked, then smiled, as he watched as his words sink in. "You're married?" Andrew queried, a second before his sister said exactly the same thing. "We've been married for six weeks tomorrow" he announced. "We wanted to keep everything a secret for a while." and he reached out to take Francesca's hand. There was a burst of talk from Sam and Andy, and Francesca saw her sister-in-law's face. The expression on it was one of surprise, and she knew that Theresa hadn't thought she would ever marry. She didn't say anything however, and received the congratulations of her siblings, and knew they were sincere. "Tell us everything" her sister commanded, and Francesca did just that. When she came to the end of her story, there was a lot of talk and laughter, and they all went into the dining room to have their meal. "So where are you living Fran? You've never given us your new address." Andy asked, when they had eaten and Dominic laughed. "It's the same as it always was. Remember, I bought your house" Andy looked stunned. "I

honestly didn't remember." he said, "We didn't have much to do with each other apart from signing papers in the solicitor's office." he said. "I knew I'd seen you before when I was introduced as your new registrar, but I couldn't remember where from."

"Andy, the prospect of becoming a father is addling your brains" Sam said, with a laugh, and they all joined in. "I knew who he was, the minute I saw him again, but Fran had never met him, because she was never with us at the same time, when we all signed the paperwork in the solicitor's office." She looked at her sister "How did you two meet, anyway?"

"She was running back to the hospital, and she trod all over me, when we bumped into each other. Then we met again, after she'd saved my stepfather's life, and I invited her out for a drink." He smiled at Francesca and took her hand. "She had no idea I'd been appointed to work in the hospital, so I would take her out to restaurants quite a way away from the hospital, so there wouldn't be any chance of being recognised by anybody who knew me. I was going to tell her one evening, after we'd been out, and I'd stopped in a lay-by, had literally opened my mouth to tell her, when my mobile rang, and it was Andrew, telling me about the train crash, and told me that I was needed urgently. I didn't have a chance to tell her after that, until we met on the ward a day or so afterwards, and he introduced us, not knowing that we knew each other already. That was a bit of a tricky moment, I can tell you. I didn't know if she'd want to continue seeing me, because I hadn't told her who I was. And straight after that, her phone was stolen, and she couldn't get in touch with me, I couldn't contact her, because I didn't get given her number, and thank goodness that Samantha got a phone call from her, when she was staying in York." He turned to her, "Why York of all places? You never did tell me." She grinned. "I was upset." she said. "I'd passed my exams, but nobody from my group was around to help me celebrate, they'd all gone home, I couldn't get in contact with any of you lot," and she gestured around her, "and then I got told I wasn't able to stay in the nurses home for my leave, which is what I'd intended doing, as I didn't have anywhere else to go. So, I thought, blow it, packed a case, and went to the station, and the first train indicated was going to York, so I bought a ticket and went there. I'd been there with Mum, and enjoyed it, but it wasn't the same, without her."

"It was my fault that Andy didn't have your number" Theresa spoke softly. "I'm really sorry Fran. I'd been out shopping, and when I came back, there was the message on the machine. I listened, went to replay it to take down the number, and pressed the wrong button, and wiped out the message. I'd received another phone call since then, so I couldn't listen to the last number dialled, and when I realised what I'd done, I didn't dare tell Andy. I thought that you would have given Sam the number as well, and I hoped she'd pass it on. It was only when Andy came home from the hospital, and told me that Dominic was going frantic trying to contact you, that I realised you were out of contact with everybody, and I didn't dare confess. When you phoned Sam again, and gave her the new number and Andy came home

and asked me what had happened, I confessed everything. He wasn't too pleased, as you can imagine, but he's done the same thing when he's been trying to listen to a message – wiped it, before he can listen again. We're going to have to get a different answer machine, one where we can't do that." she looked at Andrew as she spoke, and Fran realised that she had misjudged her sister-in-law, "Don't worry Theresa" she said now, "It all got sorted out and there's no harm done."
"Thank goodness you eventually managed to contact Samantha" Theresa said "I'm sorry for everything." Francesca nodded, and Dominic smiled at her. "Oh, don't worry, I'd have made sure I saw her again. Once I'd found her, I wasn't going to let her go again." and he kissed her hand. Andy smiled, then his face fell. "Hey, that means that my boss is also my brother-in-law" he said, and they all laughed, until he picked up his glass. "A toast" he said, "A toast to Fran and Dominic. I hope they're going to be very happy" and everybody toasted them. "Thank you" said Dominic, and changed the subject. "But what are we going to do about Maggie Lewis? I've never given her any encouragement to think that she means anything to me. Her obsession is not only embarrassing, its causing problems in theatre. As Andrew knows, I want to start doing more work with children, repairing birth defects, and a lot of it is very specialised work, and I will need to have a few nurses who know what to do. I can't just have one nurse who can scrub for me, especially as she's getting older. And as for the way she's treating Francesca, I'm wondering if

there's something wrong with her, apart from her jealousy. She's not passing on messages, she's keeping us apart at work, not allowing her into the Orthopaedic Theatres at all, and Francesca has got to know how to do some Orthopaedic operations, in case she has to scrub when she's on a late duty."

"Something is going to have to be said to Miss Elliot," said Samantha. "She's obviously aware of the situation now, after this afternoon's episode, but I think perhaps she needs to be told the entire situation. Perhaps you could go and see her tomorrow, and tell her," she suggested to Dominic, but he shrugged. "Did she say she'd see you tomorrow?" he asked Francesca and she nodded, before she spoke. "The trouble is, I don't want to be the one to tell her everything. It smacks of being a tell-tale, but I don't know what else to do."

"I'll talk to her" Dominic said. "When she calls you to see her tomorrow, let me know what she says, then I'll make an appointment to have a word with her. Just tell her exactly what happened today, tell her that Sister Lewis doesn't appear to like you at all, and mention that she's not passing on any messages, and listen to what she suggests. I'll tell her the rest of it, when I can."

"One of the nurses, Annie, said that Maggie told her she'd been getting a lot of very bad headaches recently." Francesca said, and both Andrew and Dominic looked at her in surprise. "Has she seen anybody about them?" Andy asked, but Francesca shook her head. "No, Annie said that she won't go and see anybody."

"Is Annie on duty tomorrow?" Dominic asked, and

Francesca nodded. "She's meant to be in General theatres tomorrow. She told me she was having to do an early duty after her day off, and a late duty before, and also that her days off had been split, and she wasn't very happy about it. She said that the off duty recently has become very odd, occasionally some people only get given one day a week off, and they have to ask her for their second day, and very frequently, they don't get two days together. The staff nurses are meant to have a long weekend off every four weeks, but it doesn't always happen, and a couple of the girls were moaning about that. And she's not been granting their leave applications either, tells them it's not convenient, when there's no reason why they shouldn't have leave." Dominic looked around the table. "Does that sound to anybody else, as if there's a medical problem?" he asked, and everybody nodded. "I wonder if we can find out when people started to notice that her grip on the department was slipping?" Andy said. "Fran, I'll phone Annie tomorrow morning, and ask her if we can meet, and maybe I'll be able to find out a bit more about this. I don't think Maggie would allow Dominic to meet up with Annie, because she's unmarried after all."

"If she is ill, then it would explain a lot, wouldn't it?" she said. "But it must have started soon after I had had my interview, which was about 4 months ago. She was fine at the interview, and then told Miss Lines that she was pleased I wanted to work in theatres, and she was looking forward to having me back." She grinned at her husband. "When did she become obsessed with you?" she asked and he smiled at the memory. "She showed interest the first time I was shown round the department" he said, and deliberately changed the subject. "But we can't do anything about it tonight, so let's forget about the woman, and talk about other things. Theresa, are you looking forward to being a mum? And when are you due? Andy has told me, but I'm sorry, I can't remember." The talk turned to Theresa and Francesca was glad he had changed the subject. By the time the evening ended and she and Dominic had taken Sam back to her flat, and gone to their own house, her thoughts had returned to the following day, and what was going to be said by Miss Elliot. She was silent as they went inside, and Dominic looked at her. "Okay," he said, as he took her in his arms. "What's the problem?"

"I don't know whether Miss Elliot is going to want to speak to me on my own tomorrow, or whether Sister is going to insist on being there as well, and if she is, what am I going to say to her?" she was almost crying, for she didn't know if she would be able to tell the nursing officer exactly what had happened, without the Sister giving her side of the story, and putting her in the wrong. "I hope she'll want to see you on your own" Dominic said, as he cuddled her close. "You can always ask to see her alone, if Maggie Lewis insists that she wants to be involved as well. Lena Elliot always strikes me as being very level-headed, and willing to listen to her nurses, and you heard Samantha tonight – she'll always do her best for her staff." He grinned at her, as he kissed the end of her nose. "If Maggie Lewis insists on being present, ask if I can be invited as well, and that will probably show Lena Elliot how she behaves when I'm present." Francesca smiled, and Dominic kissed her. "Come on," he said now, "let's go upstairs, have a good night's sleep, and you'll feel ready for anything tomorrow." And he led her towards the staircase. "I might have something for you, that will allow you to sleep well" he said as they went, and knowing what he meant, Francesca smiled as she allowed herself to be guided up the stairs.

When she arrived in the theatre unit the following day, she was greeted by Steph and Annie, who were in the changing room. They both asked her if she was okay. "We didn't hear everything" Steph said, "We heard Miss Elliot telling you to go home, and then there were raised voices in the office. Finally, Maggie Lewis stamped out of the office, saying she'd sort it all out today, and Miss Elliot disappeared. So what happened? I've been asked to tell you to go and see Miss Elliot at 10.00 am today, and she says she'll see Sister Lewis after that. If Maggie Lewis wants to accompany you to Miss Elliot's office, then you are to say that she wants to see you alone."
"Thank goodness" breathed Francesca, as she got changed into theatre scrubs. "I wasn't looking forward to having her in the same office, when I was talking to Miss Elliot." she smiled at Steph, and told her everything that had happened the previous afternoon. "Thanks for telling me" the senior nurse said. "You'd better not scrub for the first case this morning, as you've got an appointment." Francesca accompanied the two senior staff nurses into the

corridor, and went to look at the work list. She was due to work with Steph that morning anyway, and there were enough staff to ensure that her absence wouldn't be missed. "Did you enjoy your dinner party last night?" Steph asked, as they went into theatre, and she nodded. "It was great to catch up with my sister and brother again, especially as I wasn't able to celebrate with them when I passed my exams. My phone had been stolen, and although I'd told them of my new number, for various reasons, they didn't get it. I was a bit upset as you can imagine."

"Did you manage to celebrate with anybody?" Steph asked. "I remember our group had a massive party when we got our results."

"No" she said, and explained about the late arrival of her results, and the fact that all her group had gone by the time she received them. "And to top it off," she said with a smile, "Having got my results on the Saturday morning, I was then told on the Saturday afternoon, that I was required to move out of the nurses home, immediately, because my room was required for the new intake of girls, and my new room wasn't ready."

"That's ridiculous! So where did you go?" Steph asked, and Francesca smiled as she told her. "York. I'd been there before, with my mother, when I was helping her with some research," and she told her about her mother, the book, and the research she'd done, before she continued. "I had to find somewhere to stay, I couldn't contact Sam or Andy, and we'd sold my parents' house just before my results came through, so I didn't have anywhere else

I could go.”
“Oh Fran, you poor thing” Steph said. They had been busy, getting sets of instruments ready for the cases, when the door was flung open, and Sister Lewis stood in the doorway. “So, you've had the nerve to come back on duty” she spat at Francesca. “Miss Elliot wants to see you at 10.00 am, and I will be accompanying you, to make sure that you tell her the truth about your behaviour yesterday. I don't think you are suitable for work in this department, and I shall be telling her that. “
“You can tell her what you like” Francesca said. “But you won't be accompanying me, because she wants to see me alone. She'll see you after she's seen me.”
“I will accompany you” Sister Lewis stated, and Francesca's heart sank. Stephanie spoke then, “Sister, I'm sorry, but Miss Elliot wants to see Fran on her own. When she gets back from the office, then you are to go and see her.”
“How dare you?” Sister Lewis took a deep breath, as she asked her deputy, “How dare you question my decisions?”
“I'm not questioning your decisions Sister” Steph said firmly, “I'm telling you what Miss Elliot wants to happen. She has asked me to make sure that Fran goes on her own to see her.”
“Nonsense” said Sister. “I will accompany her, and make sure she knows what exactly happened. You'd better get on with your work Nurse Evans.” and she turned and went out of theatre. “Don't worry Fran” Steph said quietly after the woman had left the theatre. “She's going to be held up by some of the surgeons' asking her questions. We've arranged it

among ourselves, so she won't be able to go with you." Francesca smiled at the other girl. "Thanks Steph." she said quietly. "My brother and Mr. Cavanagh were discussing what happened yesterday, and they want to know when she started behaving so unreasonably. Andy was going to phone Annie this morning and have a word with her." Steph thought for a while. "She's got a lot worse in the last few weeks" she said. "She was always so reasonable about things, but it was just before Mr. Cavanagh started that she began to be a bit 'off' if you know what I mean? The off duty wasn't done properly, or if she had done it, people weren't getting their requests, and we certainly didn't get our long weekends that we've always had in the past. She started insisting that all holidays had to be booked by the end of May, otherwise we'd lose them, and when I queried that with Miss Elliot, she told me that it's not true. We are free to book our holidays whenever we like."

"Annie told me that Sister has had some very bad headaches recently and Mr. Cavanagh wondered if it might be a factor. He was going to look into it, and he said that he will be making an appointment to go and see Miss Elliot and explain everything that has happened since he got here, and tell her about Sister's behaviour."

"He's nice, isn't he?" Steph said, and Francesca smiled as she agreed with her.

She was shown into the Nursing Officer's office by the secretary, who had strict instructions not to admit Sister Lewis if she showed up. "Now Fran" the older woman said quietly, "I understand there are quite a few things that have been happening, or not happening since you started working in theatres, and I would like you to tell me about them. Don't worry about being disloyal. I'm not going to think anything less of you, for telling me exactly what's happening, but some things can't be ignored. What occurred yesterday? Shall we start with that?"

Francesca told her everything that had happened since she started work in the department, including the fact that the senior staff had been instructed not to allow her to even enter the Orthopaedic theatre despite the fact that she had to be able to do Orthopaedics if the need arose. She told her that both her sister and brother had at various times, asked Sister to pass on messages, but that she had never received any of them, and finally, she told her of the way that her off duty was changed the day before, and told her why she thought that Sister Lewis had changed it. "How do you know about the message your brother gave to Sister?" she was asked, and Francesca smiled. "I heard him telling her. He had asked her if he might give me a message, but she told him I wasn't available, despite the fact that she hadn't even looked to see if I was free. I was actually on my way to the coffee room when Andy came in, so I listened to the message, which was to the effect that Mr. Cavanagh would give me a lift to Andy's house, and I should be waiting at the entrance to the nurses home at a certain time, but Sister never passed the message on In fact, I saw Mr. Cavanagh after that, and he told me he'd sent the message, and the following morning, she told me that she'd changed my off duty." "But why should she do that?" Miss Elliot asked her, and Francesca laughed and decided she had to tell the nursing officer everything. "Because she's absolutely obsessed with Mr. Cavanagh. She won't let anybody else scrub for him at all, she works every one of his on-call duties, and every weekend when he's on call. She won't let any unmarried nurse into his theatre either, just in case he gets interested in them. The other surgeons laugh about it. He reckons it's embarrassing. When he was told about it last night, he reckoned that it was because she didn't want anybody else to have time alone with him. Goodness knows what will happen when he decides to have a holiday." She had just finished talking, when there was an outburst outside in the secretary's office and the office was nearly flung off its hinges, as Sister Lewis walked in. "She's telling lies," she burst out and Miss Elliot shook her head. "Sit down Sister" she commanded. "Staff Nurse Hallett, you may go back to theatres. Please don't talk to anybody about our meeting." Francesca stood up, but Sister Lewis leapt forward to hold onto her arm and stop her leaving. "She's a liar." she was screaming. "She's trying to stop my relationship with Dominic Cavanagh. I've seen her, I've seen her with him, laughing with him, holding his hand. She's evil.", and she drew back her arm, and tried to grasp Francesca's throat and when Francesca moved her head out of the way, she smacked Francesca around the face several times. The nursing officer was on her feet, trying to stop the senior nurse from assaulting Francesca, but it was a struggle, and

Francesca was trying to escape from the woman's grasp on her arm, but she could feel the other woman's fingernails digging in. The pain was bad, and she gasped and cried out. “Sister, let her go” Miss Elliot said loudly, and feeling the woman's grip lessen slightly, Francesca tried to get out of the office. She reached the door, but was pulled back by Sister Lewis, who grasped her arm tightly, dug her fingers in once more, and smacked her face again. Francesca was intent on escaping and gasped in relief, as Dominic opened the door. “What on earth?” he said, and Francesca, in tears after the assault, reached out and put her hand on his arm. “She's gone mad” she said. Dominic looked around him. “Let go of my Dominic.” Maggie Lewis screamed at her. “Don't touch him.” and she slapped Francesca again. “What on earth is happening?” he asked Miss Elliot, but it was Maggie Lewis who finally let go of Fran's arm and ran to put her arms around him. “Dominic darling, look after me. She's a liar. She's been telling Lena Elliot loads of lies about me.” She was holding him tight, and Dominic tried to push her away, but the woman was very strong, and he couldn't break her grip. “Somebody ring Dave Drummond, and tell him to come here immediately, and bring a sedative. It's urgent.” and seeing that Miss Elliot was busy trying to disengage the woman's grasp, Francesca swiftly made the phone call, and waited for one of the medical staff to appear. Within minutes, Dr. Drummond, the senior medical consultant arrived, took one look at the situation, and took a syringe from his pocket. “I'll give her this Dominic” he said quietly, and plunged the syringe into Sister Lewis's arm. There was a short delay before the medication worked, and Dominic was finally able to get the woman to relax her grasp on him, and seat her on a chair. "What's been happening?" Dr. Drummond asked, and Dominic, Francesca and Lena Elliot, told him everything that had happened that morning. Dominic told him about the woman's obsession with him, and Dr. Drummond looked worried. "I think we'll get her down to Casualty" he said, "and then we can sort things out. How long has this obsession been going on?"

"Since I arrived about 12 weeks ago, but apparently her behaviour has changed dramatically in the last 16 weeks. She told one of the nurses in her department that she's been having some very bad headaches recently."

"Has she?" Dr. Drummond said quietly, "I'll contact the Neurological surgeons and get them involved" he said quietly. "Staff Nurse, could you phone Accident Department and ask them to bring a trolley up here, but before you do, did she hurt you badly?" Dominic was looking at the red marks on her face and neck. "I take it she attacked you before I came?" he asked and she nodded. "She was holding my arm really tightly as well, her fingernails were digging in, and that's really painful, and it's bleeding a bit as well." His face darkened, and he stared at the woman, who was slumped on the chair he had guided her to. "Go and ring for a trolley" he ordered, "then I'm going to take you home." She had gone to do as he told her, before going back into the office, where Dr. Drummond was examining Maggie Lewis.

"I think Francesca needs to go home. I don't think she's going to be fit to work for the rest of the day." he told Miss Elliot. "I'll take her and make sure she's alright, then I'll come back and have a chat, if that would be okay?" His tone indicated that he didn't much care if it was okay or not, and Miss Elliot seemed to sense that. "Are you off duty this weekend Nurse Hallett?" she asked, and when Francesca nodded, she smiled. "Try to have a good and peaceful weekend" she said. "Come back on Monday, and we'll have a chat then. Take her home Mr. Cavanagh, and make sure she's okay." and Dominic led Francesca out of the office, and up to the theatre unit to get changed, before he took her back downstairs, put her in the car and drove her home.

Chapter Nine

"She's not at all well, is she?" Francesca said, as Dominic drew up outside the house, and he shook his head. "I don't think she is." he said quietly, "but let's get you inside and I'll have a look at your arm, and make sure she's not done any permanent damage to you." He led her inside the house, and when Mrs. Bradley came to see why he was at home at that time of day, he asked for coffee to be bought to the sitting room. "I think you need something else before you have coffee" he said, and went over to the drinks cabinet, to get her a drink. "That's Brandy" he said with a grin. "Drink up, because I think you might need it." She was shaking, but sipped the drink, and gradually the shaking stopped. Francesca was sitting back on the settee when he began to examine her, and gasped, as he saw the amount of blood that had run down her arm. "How the hell did she do that?" he asked, as he began to clean the wound site. He had seen that there were several deep indentations where the finger nails had dug in, in several places, when she had altered her grip. He cleaned and dressed the wounds, and turned his attention to her face, which was bruised, where she had been repeatedly slapped and noticed the scratches on her neck, where Maggie had tried to grab her, before she had moved her head away. "She really had a go at you, didn't she?" he said, and kissed her gently. Mrs. Bradley had bought in a tray of coffee for them both, and he poured a cup for her. "Drink that my darling" he said, and held it for her. Francesca took a couple of sips, then started to talk,

as the shock began to wear off. “She was calling you Dominic darling” she said, “and before you arrived, she was telling Miss Elliot that I was trying to stop you from seeing her. She said she'd seen us together, laughing and holding hands, and I was trying to stop your relationship with her.”
“As you said, she's not well.” Dominic said. “It sounds to me as if she's got something wrong in her brain. Dr. Drummond will refer her to the Neuro surgeons, and they'll do some scans, and see if there's a medical problem. Perhaps it could be cured by surgery, but I'll find out when I get back.”
Francesca had drunk her coffee by now, and she put the cup back on the tray. Dominic stood up, and she looked at him. “Are you going back now?” she said, but he shook his head. “No, my darling, not yet. I think you need some rest. I'm going to to take you upstairs, and give you something to make you sleep, and when you're asleep and resting, I'll go back and see Lena Elliot. I’ll be back when you're awake again. Hopefully by then, everything will have been sorted out, and we can decide what we're going to do.” He helped her to her feet, and led her upstairs. He pulled the bedclothes back, and helped her off with her clothes. “Lay down my darling, and take this” and he produced a bottle of liquid and gave her a dose of it. “That will send you off to sleep,” he said, “but I'm not going to leave you alone for a while. I'll wait until you are asleep,” and he bent his head to kiss her. The kiss lengthened, but he didn't try to touch her intimately, but instead lay beside her, holding her close. After a short while, her eyes closed, her breathing became regular, and when he

was satisfied she was sound asleep, he carefully sat up, and slid off the bed, dropped a kiss on her hair, before he covered her with a blanket, and went downstairs again. Mrs. Bradley was waiting for him, in the hallway. "What on earth happened?" she asked, and Dominic took her into the sitting room, and told her the events of the morning. "I've given her a strong sedative, and it's now taken effect. I want her to sleep for as long as she can, so please don't try and wake her. I'll be home as soon as I can, and I'll be able to sit with her until she's awake again. I'm hoping that this whole episode will be forgotten about as soon as it can. I'll be going back to talk to the nursing officer, and find out what she's going to do."

"I'll keep an eye on her Mr. Dominic. Such a lovely young lady, your wife is. I'm glad that somebody senior is now going to look into the affair, and hopefully get something sorted out. The situation can't continue like this."

"I totally agree Mrs. Bradley. I'll just check on Francesca, and then I'll get back to the hospital. I'll see you later on."

He ran upstairs to check on Francesca, and found that she was still deeply asleep, lying where he had left her. Poor Francesca, he thought, as he straightened the blanket, and bent to kiss her forehead. Maggie Lewis was obviously ill, but everything had remained hidden, until Francesca's arrival had set off a train of events. He shut the door quietly behind him, ran down the stairs again, and went out to the car, to drive back to the hospital.

He walked into the A&E department, and the first person he saw was Dr. Drummond. “What's happened?” he asked, but the older man took him by the arm and led him away. “She started to rouse from the sedative, really quickly, and we've had to give her some really strong knock out drops to get her to lie quietly. She keeps on asking where you are, and why you haven't come to see her. Are you sure you've never given her any encouragement?”
Dominic shook his head. “I met her for the first time I was taken around the department when I arrived, and she was really friendly then. Since then, she's always scrubbed for every case I did. It's been embarrassing as well as difficult. But I've never encouraged her. Why would I when I was busy with a new relationship of my own?”
“I take it, you mean Staff Nurse Hallett? Why else would Maggie Lewis get such a fixation about the girl taking you away from her?”
“Yes, Francesca and I have been out together on quite a few occasions.” He was deliberately not saying anything to anybody about their marriage, but knew their relationship would come out before too long. “Maggie Lewis must have seen us when we were together.” He hesitated, “I've been wondering whether she's got a tumour? That would have altered her perception about us, and could have started off this ridiculous infatuation.”
“Yes, I'd already thought of that.” Dr. Drummond nodded his head. “I've already contacted the Neurological Surgeons, and one of them is with her at the moment. I believe they are going to send her to CT scanner in a short while. Perhaps you'd better

go and talk to Lena Elliot about the situation. She said you would see her when you returned."
"I'll go and do that now." he half turned away, then faced the other man again. "Thank you for your help. I never thought when I phoned you this morning, that I'd require your assistance so soon."
"That's okay my boy. I was glad to help. Is Nurse Hallett, okay?"
"She's got some very nasty wounds on her arm, where Maggie put her fingernails in, and her face is going to be bruised where she was slapped repeatedly, but I've dressed the wounds, and given her a sedative, and she's asleep, and hopefully she'll stay asleep until I get home." He smiled at his colleague, not realising he had given away the fact that they were living together. "I'll go and see Lena Elliot. Would you keep me up to date please?"
"Of course I will. See you later." and he watched as Dominic walked out of the department and out of sight, before he turned and went back to look after his patient.

When Dominic was admitted to Lena Elliot's office, the older woman stood up, and shook his hand. "Thank you for all your help" she said. "It was a bit worrying there for a while, as you can imagine. Do you have any further information?"
"Sister Lewis is being seen by the Neuro. surgeons at the moment, and they will be sending her for a CT scan very soon, or so Dr. Drummond tells me."
"And how is Francesca?"
"I've given her a sedative, dressed the wounds that Maggie inflicted on her, and left her sound asleep in

bed. I think she'll be okay, but obviously it was a nasty experience for her" and he told her about the wounds on her arm, and face. "I had no idea that Maggie was behaving as irrationally as she obviously was doing. I had noticed the off duty wasn't being done properly, but I didn't give it a thought." Lena Elliot looked worried. "She's always been a bit highly strung, but she's never given any indication that there is anything wrong with her. But I can't understand how she would have gained the impression that you and she were an item."

"Nor can I" he said. "The only contact I have with her, is when she's scrubbed for me, and when I've told her what operations I need to get done. It was a few weeks ago, that Stephanie Evans told me that she was obsessed with me, and since then I've noticed the way, she's acted towards me. I must admit, I had no idea she felt that way before then. But Steph Evans did tell me that she felt sorry for any woman who I was seeing, if she ever came to theatres because Maggie would probably treat them very badly, and as I've been seeing Francesca for a few weeks, it's obvious that Maggie has seen us together, and is venting her frustration onto Francesca."

"I'm not being personal, but I wondered, what exactly is your relationship with Nurse Hallett? I just wondered there is anything in the relationship that would upset Sister further, if she returns to work quite soon?" Dominic hesitated, then knew he was going to have to tell her. "Please keep this information to yourself, but Francesca and I were married a few weeks ago." he said. "We were trying

to keep it secret for a while, just because she's only just started out on her career, and I'm a consultant, but we didn't want to wait. In fact," he smiled at the memory, "we only told her sister and brother at the dinner party, last night."
"Oh congratulations" Lena Elliot said, and smiled at him. "But I can understand that it might cause a problem if Sister returns to work."
"I don't think she'll be back at work for quite a while" Dominic said. "From the way she behaved, and from what Dr. Drummond said, we think she could have a tumour. If it's removed, she'll have to be off work for quite a long time." Miss Elliot looked shocked. "I will go down to A&E and see if there's anything I can do" she said. "I won't tell anybody about you and Nurse Hallett, and I can only thank you again for your assistance. Maggie was so strong; I couldn't break her grip on Francesca's arm. She was distracted by your appearance, which is why she eventually let her go."
"Have you told anybody in theatres about what happened?" he asked, but she shook her head. "No, I've told them that Sister isn't well, and is receiving medical treatment, and that Francesca was so upset about it, I've sent her home and she'll be back in on Monday."
"I won't say anything." he said, and they parted company, he to return to his office, and Miss Elliot to go to A&E.

When he returned home, later that afternoon, he ran lightly upstairs and looked at Francesca. She was just waking from her sleep, but there were

several bruises developing on one side of her face, and it was swollen, as was her arm which was very bruised as well. He lay beside her, to hold her as she woke, and was rewarded by her kiss, when she opened her eyes. She snuggled against him, then remembered what had happened, and tried to pull away, but he stopped her, and kissed her, gently at first, then deeper, and he could feel her relaxing.
"What's happened?" she asked, when he lifted his head. "How is she? Still thinking that you're her ideal man?"
"No," he held her tight. "She was sent for a CT scan by the Neuro surgeons, and she's got a massive tumour in her frontal lobe, which is obviously upsetting her reasoning. They've got her listed for surgery tomorrow, and they're hoping it's not malignant. They were awaiting results when I came home, so I'll find out later. One of the Neuro boys will phone me, and keep me updated." He kissed her again, his mouth hard against hers. "She wanted to see me, but I kept out of her way, because the Neuro surgeons thought that was sensible. She's off sick now, and she will be for quite a while. How do you feel?"
"My face is sore and my arm hurts. How tightly was she holding on to me?"
"Well, from the depth of the wounds on your arm, I would say very tightly. Her nails were digging into you. It's bruised as well as cut. You were bleeding quite freely if you can remember. I've phoned Andrew and he's coming to see us this evening, so I can tell him what's happened. I've been forced into secrecy at work, so I didn't want to tell him there in

case anybody overhears us."
"Nobody will keep that a secret" Francesca said, "Everybody will know that she needs surgery."
"I don't mean the surgery" he said, "I mean the way she attacked you in Miss Elliot's office this morning. Your colleagues have been told that you were so upset by the scene, that you were taken home. I'm sorry, but I've had to tell Miss Elliot about our marriage. She said she won't tell anybody, but I'm wondering now, if perhaps we shouldn't keep it a secret anymore."
"We've had a few weeks of deceiving everybody, haven't we? It's been fun, but as you say, perhaps we ought to tell people" she smiled at him, then winced, as her face hurt. He bent his head to kiss her again. The kiss grew longer, and before she lost all reason, she knew she was going to enjoy telling everybody about their marriage.

That evening, Dominic took a phone call from the hospital, "That was Robert Soames, the Neuro surgeon. They can't get a definite answer to whether the tumour is malignant or benign, but they'll find out during the surgery tomorrow. Apparently, they've had to keep her sedated, with really strong drugs, because she keeps on screaming at the ward staff to let her see me. She's tried to attack one of the female nurses already, and they've got a male nurse specialising her at the moment, because she's so strong, they dare not leave a female with her. They reckon she could do a lot of damage."
"It's not your fault" Francesca said. "You must have arrived, just when the tumour started to grow and

her emotions were damaged. Dominic, don't beat yourself up about this. Despite everything, I feel sorry for her."
"So do I" he said, "but I also feel sorry for the nurses who are having such a bad time with her at the moment." he deliberately changed the subject. "So, what delectable dish has Mrs. Bradley left for us tonight?" Francesca smiled as she started to dish up the meal, and they were soon eating it, and clearing away afterwards. They had just finished, and she had taken the dirty dishes into the kitchen, when the doorbell rang, and Dominic went to answer it, and found Andy and Theresa on the doorstep. "Come in" he invited, and led them into the sitting room, calling to ask Francesca to make coffee. Dominic was showing them around, telling him about the changes he had made, and Theresa, who hadn't often been to the house, was impressed with it. As she bought the tray with the coffee pot and cups on, into the room, Andrew looked properly at his sister, and saw the bruises on her face and the dressings on her arm. "What the hell has he done to you?" he demanded, and both Francesca and Dominic started to laugh, although Francesca winced as she smiled. "This wasn't Dominic" she insisted. "Sit down, have your coffee, and we'll tell you all about it." The telling didn't take long, and Andrew sat open mouthed, as Dominic told him everything. "I didn't realise she was so ill" he said and Theresa was shaking her head. "Oh, poor Maggie" she said. "She doesn't deserve to be so unwell. Everybody got on well with her, and she's got a lot of friends in the hospital, who will want to see her, and make sure she's going to be

okay."
"She's not my favourite person at the moment," Francesca said dryly. "It hurts to smile, my arm is very sore and bruised, and although I know she's not well, and probably didn't mean it, I don't feel that I want anything to do with her. Thank goodness for Dominic turning up when he did, otherwise, she might have killed me. She was going for my throat, to try and strangle me, before she grabbed my arm to hold me in place, and started smacking my face. Miss Elliot couldn't get her off me, and I couldn't move away, because she was holding my arm so tight. Her nails were digging in, and I've got lots of wounds in my arm where she held me" and she indicated the dressings on her arm and the gouges on her neck. Theresa winced as she looked at them. "I hadn't realised how serious it obviously was" Andrew said. "You say she's going for surgery tomorrow?" Dominic nodded. "They won't be able to say if the tumour is benign, until they send it off for testing. I really hope it is."
"So do I" Andrew and Theresa spoke together, and Francesca nodded. When her brother and sister-in-law had left, she stretched. "I think I'll have an early night, despite the fact that I've been asleep all afternoon" she said, with a smile, and Dominic laughed. "In other words, you want to go to bed?" he said, but she shook her head. "I'm going to have a bath, and relax, and then I'll go to bed and read for a while, before I go to sleep." Dominic smiled as he held her close. "Let's go and have a bath together" he suggested, "and then I know exactly how to relax you." She laughed at his words, and leaving him to

lock up and turn the lights out, she ran upstairs.

They spent the weekend together quietly, although they did phone his stepfather on Saturday afternoon, to give him the news about their wedding, and Francesca was welcomed with such enthusiasm, that she felt very glad. Later that evening, his phone rang, and on answering it, he listened for a while, then said, "Oh thank goodness. I'll let Francesca know." before he disconnected. "That was Rob. Soames. He's operated, and removed all the tumour, and although they've got to wait for a couple of days before they get results, he reckoned that the tumour is benign, and she'll make a full recovery." Francesca breathed a sigh of relief. "Thank goodness" she said, glad to know that the woman stood a good chance of a happier future.

On Monday morning, she walked into the theatre unit and went to get changed. Her face was still bruised, but the swelling had gone down now, and she had told everybody who asked, that she had fallen and bruised her face. She didn't think a lot of people believed that, but nobody queried it until Steph said quietly to her "Does the bruising on your face and arm, have anything to do with your meeting with Miss Elliot on Friday morning? It just seems so strange that Maggie Lewis went off sick and you were sent home, just after she stormed off to see Miss Elliot." Francesca nodded and Steph said quietly, "don't worry, I won't say anything else. She really does hate you, doesn't she?" Francesca nodded again, but knew she had to be fair to the woman. “I don't think she did hate me” she said, “but circumstances have changed everything. I promise I'll explain as soon as I can” she continued, and Steph nodded and left her to get ready for the case she was going to scrub for.

The rest of the week that followed seemed to be unreal for Francesca. The department was a lot happier, now that Sister Lewis wasn't on duty, and Stephanie Evans was in charge, and now known by her correct title, and Fran had started to enjoy herself at work again. She had gone into the hospital, done everything she was told to do, then gone home again, spending as much time with Dominic as she was able to do. She was on a day off on Thursday, for she was going to work the weekend, and it was just after lunch, when the phone rang, and on answering, found that it was Miss Elliot. “Fran, I've had a request from Sister Lewis.” she began. “She's doing very well, she's out of bed, recovering slowly, but when I visited her yesterday, she asked if I would contact you, and ask if you could see your way to visiting her. She said she needs to talk to you.”
“I don't think so” Francesca said quietly. “The last time I saw her, she tried very hard to kill me, and I don't really fancy visiting her, so she can repeat the experience.”
“She's changed completely” Miss Elliot said quietly. “She's calmer, she knows what she did, and remember she wasn't really in the right frame of mind to know what she was doing. She's also been told that the tumour is benign, so hopefully she'll be

okay from now on. Would you visit her, providing I was with you, and also if there were a couple of hefty male nurses around, to stop her, if she did try to attack you again?"
"Has she really changed that much?" Francesca asked, and the other woman answered in the affirmative. "The first thing she did after she woke up and was completely lucid again, was to apologise for causing so many problems. When I visited her soon afterwards, she told me she was sorry for having acted as she did. I did mention Mr. Cavanagh to her, and she said she had no idea why she had become infatuated with him. In fact, she laughed, when I reminded her that she had felt that way. She has no idea of why it had happened, but she does remember treating you badly, and would like to speak to you. Will you come and see her my dear?"
Francesca thought rapidly back to the scene in the office. "Would you definitely be present?" she asked, unwilling to see the woman on her own.
"Most definitely my dear" was the answer, and Francesca agreed. They arranged for her to go into the hospital that afternoon, and she phoned Dominic to let him know where she was going. He wasn't able to take the call, for he was operating, so she left a message in his voicemail, and went to tell the housekeeper that she was going out.

When she arrived at the hospital, she went to Miss Elliot's office, and was greeted with a smile. "Thank you for coming" the older woman said. "I know this can't be too easy for you, but I do appreciate you giving up your time like this."

Francesca accompanied the nursing officer downstairs, and as she walked into the ward, she felt a shiver run down her spine. "I'll be on hand" whispered Miss Elliot, and Francesca nodded. There were two male nurses standing close by the door of the side room, and Francesca knew that they were there for her protection, if the older woman began to behave badly. She drew in a deep breath, and opened the door of the room where Maggie Lewis was a patient. She was sitting in an armchair, a bandage around her head, and looked totally different to the virago who had attacked her nearly a week ago. She looked calm, and as Francesca opened the door, she looked up, saw her visitor, and smiled at her. "Fran" she said quietly, "thank you for coming. Please sit down." and she indicated the other chair. Francesca hesitated as she did as she had been bidden, and Maggie saw the hesitation, and smiled. "I need to apologise to you" she said and saw the surprise on Francesca's face. "I know I behaved badly to you, and I believe I injured you." she indicated the bruising that was still visible on Francesca's face and arm. "I do apologise to you for doing that. I know that I did it, but I hope you can understand that I had no control over my actions. For some reason unknown to me, I became infatuated with Mr. Cavanagh, thought that he felt the same way about me, as I did about him. His private life means nothing to me at all." she paused, then continued, "I know now, that I wasn't well, it was the tumour that was causing me to act as I did, but I didn't realise that I was unwell. But I saw you two together, and the sight of you laughing and joking together, holding hands, made me act badly towards you. I decided that I wasn't going to allow you to scrub for him, I was going to keep you on opposite duties to him, so you wouldn't have an opportunity to see him outside the hospital, and I wanted nothing more than for you to leave the theatres. I withheld messages from your sister, asking you to phone her, and on the day before I was taken so ill, I'd taken a message from your brother, telling you that Mr. Cavanagh would take you to your brother's house for a dinner party. I decided that I wasn't going to allow that, and not only failed to pass on the message, but I also decided to change your off duty, so you wouldn't be able to go to the dinner party. I'm very sorry Fran. I don't deserve it, but I would hope that you could forgive me for acting as I did. As I say, it must have been the tumour that was causing me to behave as I did, because I certainly wouldn't have wanted to interfere with your private life, and I wanted to apologise to you, for acting so badly towards you. I don't know why I fixated on Mr. Cavanagh. He certainly means nothing to me, apart from being one of the departments surgeons. I do hope my actions haven't interfered with any romantic intentions that Mr. Cavanagh had towards you?" Francesca had listened to this speech without comment, but she knew from her time in the Neurological unit, how tumours could upset the way some patients acted, and knew too, that the woman seemed to be sincere. "Yes," she said now, "I can forgive you, because you weren't acting as you had done, when I first worked in theatres, and no, you haven't interfered with the

way that Dominic and I feel towards each other."
"Would you be able to ask him if I could see him to apologise to him?" Maggie Lewis appeared quite humble. "He seems a very nice man, he was always polite to me, even when I was being so badly behaved towards him, he's a very good surgeon as well, and I hope he doesn't feel too much ill will towards me."
"He doesn't feel any ill will towards you" said Dominic from the doorway, where he had just arrived, and had been listening, and Francesca turned a smiling face towards him. Sister Lewis looked apprehensively at him, and Dominic came into the room, taking Francesca's hand into his. "I know you weren't quite yourself when you acted as you did" he said, "and I hope I will have the pleasure of getting to know the real you, when you return to your duties."
"I won't be coming back" she said. "I've talked to Lena Elliot, and I've decided to take early retirement, on health grounds. But I'm very sorry for my actions Mr. Cavanagh, and you too, Francesca. I want to apologise to you both."
"That's very kind of you." Dominic said quietly. "And I can assure you, that you haven't been able to interfere with the progress of our romance. We were married just before she started working in theatres, and we're very happy together" and he bent his head to kiss the hand he was holding.
"Married!" Sister Lewis looked astounded. "Oh, I'm so pleased for you both. Please accept my congratulations." She took Francesca's hand in hers. "You're a very good nurse my dear, and you've learnt so much about theatre work in the short time you

were working. It will be a loss to the department when you start a family and leave." Francesca looked astounded, but didn't say anything, and when it was time for her to leave, she felt sorry, as she said her farewells. "Take care my dear, and be happy. That's the main thing in life" said Maggie Lewis, as they prepared to leave. "And again, my congratulations to you both. Please keep in touch." They assured her that they would, and walked away from the ward, accompanied by Miss Elliot, who had remained in the corridor.

As they left the department, Miss Elliot turned to them both. "Congratulations" she said. "I take it, you're going to let everybody know the good news. You won't be able to keep it a secret for very long, especially in this hospital, and especially now that Maggie Lewis knows. The way that gossip seeps through the grapevine, is incredible. Maggie won't keep the news to herself, you know?"

"I know" Dominic said with a smile. "It's amazing how news goes around. When Francesca gets into work tomorrow lunchtime, I'll bet the entire theatre unit will want to know everything. Sorry Francesca, there will be lots of questions for you to answer. They will want
to know where, when, what you wore, and how many guests we had at the reception. I'll try and help if I can, but I don't think I'll be able to stop too many questions."

"Well, the last one will be an easy one to answer, won't it?" she said with a smile. "None, because we didn't have a reception."

"Didn't you?" Miss Elliot asked, and they both smiled at her. "No, we just got married in a registry office, with two witnesses, we picked at random." Dominic replied, then laughed. "I think we'll have to have a big party with everybody from theatre so they can see what you looked like on our wedding day. I'll try and sort out something this afternoon." Miss Elliot agreed, and when she went back home afterwards, Francesca knew she was very happy.

As Dominic had forecast, when she went into the hospital at lunchtime, the following day, she was surrounded by everybody who could be there, asking questions wanting to know everything about their romance, and when he entered the unit, and came to see her, more questions came thick and fast. They answered them all, as best they could, but she knew that her friends wanted more details, for she was besieged by phone calls from members of her set, so, as he had suggested, they had arranged a party. "Who do you want to invite?" he asked, but she smiled. "Everybody who can come" she said, and he agreed. It was to be held in the hospital ballroom the following weekend, and during the week before that, she was questioned and congratulated by so many people, she didn't think that there were more who wanted to know all about their romance. On the day of the party, she and Dominic had arrived early to make sure that all the arrangements were complete. They were standing quietly together as Dominic took Francesca's hands in his, and held her close to his body. "Thank you so much for becoming my wife, my darling. I love you so very much, and I'm sure that everything will be plain sailing from now on." And he bent to kiss her gently on the lips. She kissed him back, "Thank you for wanting to marry me" she said. "We've gone through so much already; I'm looking forward to the next chapter in our lives together." He wrapped her in his arms, and kissed her deeply, before they drew apart, as the first guests began to arrive, to help celebrate their happiness.

THE END

Printed in Great Britain
by Amazon

48745936R00101